"Of course there's a man in your life, darling—me!"

A collective sigh swept through the studio audience.

"Now, listen," Emily ordered. "I don't want to make waves here, but—"

"You could make a tidal wave in a dishpan, Emily, so when it comes to vulnerable males like me…"

She ignored him and looked out over the crowd. "There is absolutely nothing between Quinn and me."

The audience shrieked with laughter.

Quinn's mouth quirked. "How can you say that after last night?"

As the crowd cheered, Emily groaned inwardly. This pretend romance was definitely getting out of hand!

Leigh Michaels dreamed of being a writer from the time she was a child. She finished her first novel when she was only fourteen and a freshman in high school, and very sensibly burned it a few years later. She wrote five more—and burned all quarter-million words—before completing *The Grand Hotel* and submitting it to Harlequin in 1981. She has since written more than forty additional romances and, she says, has enough ideas to last for another hundred years or so.

She likes to hear from readers at P.O. Box 935, Ottumwa, Iowa 52501-0935.

Books by Leigh Michaels

HARLEQUIN ROMANCE
3214—THE BEST-MADE PLANS
3233—THE UNEXPECTED LANDLORD
3248—SAFE IN MY HEART
3263—TIES THAT BLIND
3275—THE LAKE EFFECT
3290—DATING GAMES
3300—A SINGULAR HONEYMOON

TRAVELING MAN
Leigh Michaels

Harlequin Books

TORONTO • NEW YORK • LONDON
AMSTERDAM • PARIS • SYDNEY • HAMBURG
STOCKHOLM • ATHENS • TOKYO • MILAN
MADRID • WARSAW • BUDAPEST • AUCKLAND

For Cary J. Hahn,
the *real* Traveling Man

ISBN 0-373-03311-7

TRAVELING MAN

Copyright © 1994 by Leigh Michaels.

CHAPTER ONE

EMILY LAMBERT PAUSED on the wide stair landing and looked out the window. At this hour of the morning, the eastern sky held only a hint of light, but the tiny flush of pink at the horizon promised a cloudless day to come. She wished she could stand there and watch the sun rise, but the watch on her wrist was ticking away relentlessly.

The house was almost silent, and she crept down the last flight of stairs to the kitchen. If she was very quiet, perhaps Gran wouldn't hear her at all.

But she caught the aroma of freshly brewed coffee just as she pushed open the swinging doors to the kitchen. "Good morning, Gran," she said almost accusingly.

A diminutive white-haired lady turned from the stove to smile at her. Her velvety brown eyes, the same shade as Emily's, sparkled in her wrinkled pink face. "You're running just a little early today, dear. You weren't trying to sneak out of the house, were you?"

Emily sighed. "Of course I was. With that cold, Gran, you shouldn't be getting up in the middle of the night to make oatmeal for me."

"It isn't the middle of the night, and you need your breakfast, dear."

"And you need your sleep," Emily grumbled.

Carrie Lambert pointed to the single place already set at the round breakfast table.

The gesture was obviously an order, so Emily gave up the argument, poured herself a cup of coffee and sat down. She shook out her linen napkin. "I must admit it smells awfully good."

Carrie spooned the steaming cereal into a bowl and carried it to the table. "Solid food," she said, sitting down across from Emily. "That's what you need, facing all that stress every day. And if you won't eat bacon and eggs..." She watched Emily spread brown sugar over the cereal and shook her head. "I can't get over seeing you leave for work looking that way."

"Well, it would be a waste of time to put on makeup, don't you think? I'd just have to strip it off again when I got to the TV station."

"Yes," Carrie said, though she sounded doubtful. "Still, leaving your hair wet like that, and wearing jeans... You don't look very professional."

"Believe me, Gran, nobody's around the station at this hour of the morning except the people whose job it is to make me look beautiful. When I go in this way, it makes them feel needed and appreciated."

Carrie didn't appear convinced. "Well, I hope whoever chose that dress you were wearing yesterday doesn't feel appreciated. It looked like a sack. You need things with a waistline to show off your tiny little middle."

Emily tried not to smile. "Next time I'll tie a camera cable around my waist."

Carrie sniffed. "Even a belt wouldn't have changed that awful shade of gray."

Emily pushed back her chair. "I've got to run, Gran."

"I'll be watching the show." Carrie tipped her cheek up for a kiss.

"My most devoted fan. The oatmeal tasted wonderful— but don't take that as encouragement to do it again. I still think you should have stayed in bed." Emily poured the rest of her coffee into a travel mug, grabbed her backpack and an old windbreaker off a hook in the back hallway and crossed the patch of still-frosty lawn to her car.

The city never slept completely, of course, but at this hour of the morning the pace was subdued. Traffic was extremely light, and it took only a few minutes to get from the Lambert house in Brookside to the south edge of Kansas City's downtown area. Still, by the time she parked her car near a nondescript, sprawling building, the eastern sky was glowing and street lamps were beginning to blink out.

Inside, the building was awash with light, and staff members were already bustling back and forth. Emily nodded and smiled at several, and turned down a corridor toward Studio B, where "Kansas City Morning" would go on the air in less than two hours. She'd catch up on the overnight news and review the guest schedule for the show, and then it would be time for makeup....

In Emily's tiny dressing room, a woman was waiting, sitting on the arm of a chair and paging though the morning newspaper. Nearby was an enormous basket full of cosmetic and beauty supplies.

Emily paused. "Am I late, Joanie?"

The woman shook her head, refolded the newspaper and slid off the arm of the chair. "Gary wants to be finished with makeup by six-thirty, so I thought I'd better start you early."

That was one of the minor privileges of being the senior host, instead of the junior one, Emily thought. Gary Bennington could set his own schedule, and the rest of the cast and crew of "Kansas City Morning"—including his cohost—worked around it.

She picked up a videotape of the previous night's news show, which had been broadcast well after she was tucked into bed, and popped it into the machine. As Joanie wrapped her in a candy-striped cape, the station logo appeared on the television screen next to the makeup mirror. Emily kept one eye on the news and the other on Joanie; the woman was very good, but she had a heavy hand with mascara and blush if no one was paying attention.

Today, however, makeup went faster than usual. Just as Joanie was rolling Emily's dark brown hair smoothly into a tight chignon, a knock sounded on the door. Before Emily could even call an answer, the door opened and Gary Bennington put his head in.

"Here's a list of subjects appropriate for chitchat today," he said abruptly, and thrust a sheet of paper at Emily. "I like her hair that way," he told Joanie. "Maybe just a few tendrils left loose around her face." Then he was gone.

Emily glanced at the neatly handwritten list and suppressed a sigh. She'd been on the show for three solid months; surely by now Gary shouldn't feel it necessary to guide and script every word she said! She was a professional, after all; she certainly wasn't going to start telling tasteless jokes on the air. But if anything, Gary seemed to be getting more controlling as the weeks went by.

His need to feel in charge wasn't surprising, in itself. "Kansas City Morning" had been Gary's show for a decade, so it was no wonder he felt responsible for every detail. And Emily wondered sometimes if he knew, by instinct if nothing else, that there were changes in the wind. He must have suspected that the producer was already looking a year or two ahead, when Gary would retire. That was why Emily had been hired, after all, to provide some continuity through all the changes that would be coming up.

But it was time to get onto the set, so she unwrapped the dress that Wardrobe had delivered. It was navy blue with a modified sailor collar. Not as bad as yesterday, of course—this one had a sleek silhouette and even a matching belt—

but Gran would have no trouble finding fault with it, Emily was sure.

The studio was already bustling when she took her place on the set with five minutes to airtime. It was a big room, with what looked like a large and comfortable living area built along one side. At the center of it was a love seat, covered in a soft nubby blue fabric. A matching club chair stood at an inviting angle by the fireplace. There was even a television set in one corner and a book on the low coffee table, completing the image of a perfect place to curl up and relax.

But of course, in a television studio, almost nothing was precisely as it appeared. The love seat was not deep and luxurious as it seemed to be; it was specially constructed with a shallow, extra-firm seat, which made it impossible to do anything but sit up straight. The fireplace was a fake, with not even a gas log to create the illusion of warmth. The television set was not a home model, but a businesslike triple monitor, which showed the same range of camera angles the director was getting in the control room. And the book had been carefully placed on the coffee table to promote tomorrow's show, when the author would be a guest on "Kansas City Morning." The center of the huge room was full of cameras and technicians and miles of cables and cords. Along the far wall were a hundred chairs, arranged like theater seats in elevated rows for the comfort of a studio audience. They were never used, however; Gary Bennington had been heard to say that broadcasting live was taking risks enough, without adding a whole lot of amateurs to the stew. That was one of the things that would change, Emily thought, when Gary retired. At least, it would change if she had anything to say about it.

Emily shifted uncomfortably on the love seat as she reviewed the first half hour's schedule, and glanced toward the control room, where the director was signaling that the show would start in thirty seconds.

Emily didn't need the warning. A sixth sense—a combination of experience and timing—had already told her that her cue was just moments away. She felt a familiar tightening in her stomach as the camera lens zoomed in on her face. She wasn't quite used to that yet, even after three months; things had been easier in radio.

She smothered the urge to check the monitor one last time to be sure every hair was in place. Being caught staring at oneself when a camera suddenly went live was the mark of an amateur—and that was the last thing Emily wanted to look like.

The red light atop the main camera blinked on. Emily smiled automatically, and from the club chair beside the fireplace, Gary launched into the long-established opening routine. First came teasers about the interviews and features to be included in the first hour, then a cut to the newsroom for an update on the national situation, then the business summary....

The first hour passed quickly, as it always did. The interviews seemed to flash by, and only during the advertising breaks could Emily glance at her notes and remind herself of what came next. Gary, on the other hand, seemed to have no trouble. She wondered sometimes if the man memorized the entire schedule each morning, down to the number of seconds allotted to each guest.

Don't get sidetracked, Emily warned herself. The studio camera wasn't focused on her at the moment, but in a minute or two it would be, just as soon as Robin Wright, in the weather room next door to Studio B, finished explaining the colder-than-normal temperatures she was predicting for overnight in the central United States. Emily shuffled her notes and put them back on the coffee table, where the low centerpiece concealed them from the camera.

Robin stumbled over the pronunciation of a local town. Emily shot a glance at Gary, who shook his head in disgust and said something under his breath.

"And that's the weather for this hour," Robin finished. "Emily?"

The red light came on, and Emily smiled into the lens. "Thanks for the warning, Robin. Should we all spend the evening covering flowers to keep them from being frozen?"

From the corner of her eye, Emily saw the monitor shift again, and Robin shook her head. "Most buds haven't opened enough to be affected by a light frost. But if you have plants that are blooming ahead of schedule, some protection might be a good idea."

Gary smiled as the camera zoomed in on him, once more the perfect host who never showed a glint of annoyance on the air. "Now for another view of the great outdoors," he said, his rich voice oozing charm as the camera zoomed in on his face. "Here's the Traveling Man, who stopped by a Kansas City park yesterday and discovered that no matter what the weather report says, the kids have decided it's spring."

The camera's red light blinked off, and on the monitor appeared the standard opening for this daily feature. A big almond-colored recreational vehicle, with the television station logo emblazoned on the side, moved briskly down a deserted highway, the hiss of tires barely audible against a lilting, cheerful theme song.

The director appeared at the edge of the set. "You wanted me, Gary?"

How did Tish know Gary wanted her? Emily had seen nothing that looked like a summons.

"If that young woman can't stop tripping over her tongue," Gary began heatedly, "we'll have to replace her. Anyone who can't pronounce 'Chillicothe' is going to be in serious trouble when she starts running into Native American names. For heaven's sake, Tish..."

Emily turned back to the monitor, biting her lip. Everyone made mistakes; she'd even heard Gary stumble a time or two. It wasn't reasonable to expect perfection in live broadcasting, so why was he wasting time over trifles?

On the screen, Quinn Randolph, better known to viewers all over the Midwest as the Traveling Man, was surrounded by a multitude of small bodies, all apparently ignoring the camera. Emily had to give Quinn some credit for that; but since she doubted that he'd found a bunch of kids who had no interest in waving at their friends on television, most of the credit had to go to the editor.

Gary Bennington had finally run out of breath.

"I'll speak to her, Gary," the director promised. "But you can't expect that no one will ever..."

The view on the monitor shifted, drawing Emily's attention back to Quinn, standing on a high point in the park and looking out over the sea of kids. "...and they have a point," he said. "Spring *is* different for kids..."

The camera came in close, filling the screen with his face. The wind ruffled his sun-streaked brown hair, and his eyes, dark hazel and surrounded by the longest and curliest black lashes Emily had ever seen on a man, sparkled mischievously.

"...kids of all ages," Quinn Randolph finished, and the camera pulled back just a bit and followed his dizzying spiral down a long slide.

"What a job," Emily muttered. "Last week he toured an ice-cream factory, this week he's playing in the park!"

At the bottom of the slide, Quinn dusted off the seat of his jeans and turned to the camera with a grin. "I'm Quinn Randolph, the Traveling Man, along with the rest of the kids at the park."

The director edged away from the set and froze in her steps as the studio camera went live once more. Emily, who had not picked up her cue from the control room, was a beat late in responding to the demand of the red light, and she hadn't entirely thought out what she was going to say. She could see Gary's frown from the corner of her eye.

At least my gaffe might take the pressure off Robin, she thought, and managed to say, "Someone asked me yesterday if Quinn lives in that RV all the time."

"That's an interesting question," Gary said smoothly. "You can talk to him about it tomorrow."

She didn't have the least idea what he meant. "Oh?"

"Quinn's going to be our guest, so we can chat with him about all his adventures. Won't that be great?" Gary's enthusiasm was apparent.

Emily didn't share it. She didn't have anything against Quinn Randolph exactly, and she didn't doubt that viewers would be interested. But the question was one of journalistic ethics; when one of the station's programs promoted another that way, it looked bad. But she could hardly get into a discussion with Gary on the air, could she?

She said weakly, "Of course. That'll be great fun," and announced the advertising break.

Gary was glowering. "That was absolutely rude, Emily. You could have shown some excitement."

"You took me by surprise. Quinn wasn't on your list of subjects."

"You're the one who's always talking about the merits of live television, then you trip over your tongue like that!" Gary snorted. "What's wrong with you?"

Emily sighed. "All right," she admitted. "It wasn't just the surprise I was reacting to. I don't think it's in good taste for the station to blow its own horn that way. It's a conflict of interest for us to interview our own people—"

"Later," Gary said curtly as the break ended. Their rundown of special features for the next day's show went smoothly, Emily remembered her special goodbye wave for Gran, and the show was over. Gary jumped out of his chair and was halfway across the studio before Emily could get up.

"I'd like to finish this discussion," she called after him.

"It's already decided. Quinn will be here tomorrow."

She looked after him in exasperation. "What's next? We start interviewing the secretaries about how much fun it is to work for exciting people like us? Then the accountants will probably want equal time, and we'll end up looking as if we're too lazy to go out and find guests who matter!"

But Gary was gone. Emily gathered up her notes, unclipped her tiny microphone and headed for her dressing room to unwind.

Robin came out of the weather room and fell into step beside her. "I suppose Gary's threatening to have my head for goofing up like that."

Emily had to bite her tongue for a moment before she could be diplomatic. "Well, it is his show, so you have to understand that he feels personally insulted if anything goes wrong, no matter how petty."

"And because he developed the format and built the audience, he owns the thing and can do no wrong?" Robin sighed.

Emily didn't answer. There was nothing she could say that would be both true and polite.

"Don't get me wrong," Robin said, "I appreciate Gary's dedication. I even admire the vision that got the show started. But that was years ago. He won't let 'Kansas City Morning' grow beyond his original concept, and it's getting absolutely geriatric. Have you seen the latest market statistics?''

Emily nodded. ''Of course I have. Still, for an independent station without a network backing us, we do very well.''

''Oh, really? Our average fan is over sixty and retired. I thought when the station hired you, we might be making a push for the younger viewer, but frankly, in three months I haven't seen much change.'' She eyed Emily with obvious curiosity.

Emily reminded herself that the plans for what ''Kansas City Morning'' might look like after Gary's departure were still firmly in the future and not open for discussion. ''What worries me,'' she said, almost to herself, ''is that it isn't like Gary to snap at people for trifles.''

''You haven't known him long, have you?''

''Not very. He's always been demanding, of course. But he's not usually rude. In the last week or two, though—''

''Maybe you're right. I'm just trying to stay out of the man's way. Do you have time for a break?''

Emily glanced at her watch. ''I've got an awful lot of reading to do.'' She brandished the book that had occupied the place of honor on the coffee table that morning.

''You've always got tons of work. It can't hurt to take ten minutes out for a doughnut.''

''I thought your doctor said you're not supposed to be eating doughnuts, Robin.''

Robin absentmindedly patted her protruding abdomen. The camera angles during the weather report had been carefully planned to conceal her figure; in person there was no hiding the fact that she was very pregnant. ''That's why I need you to keep me from indulging.'' She smiled and linked her arm with Emily's and led her down the hall to the station's commissary.

The combination cafeteria-and-lounge was unusually busy for midmorning, and nearly every table was full. Emily spotted the station manager in the farthest corner, along with Gary Bennington and the producer of "Kansas City Morning." She wondered who had called that meeting. Gary, because of his unhappiness with the flubs this morning?

Probably not, Emily decided. She was being paranoid, that was all. There were always meetings going on. Besides, the producer, Jason Manning, had told her just yesterday how delighted he was with her work. And last week he had hinted once more about the overhaul the show would get when the time was right. If he and the station manager didn't approve of her style, they wouldn't be sending her out to represent the station at public functions, either.

"That reminds me," she murmured as she picked up a bottle of sparkling water. "I've got a public appearance at noon, so I really don't have much time to chat."

Robin passed up the doughnuts—huge, gooey, chocolate-covered things—with a sigh. Instead, she selected dry toast and tea, and chose a table near the commissary door. "In that case, you really need to relax."

Emily opened the bottle and poured the water over ice. It hissed gently, and the first sip tickled her tongue. "Did you hear the bit about Gary bringing Quinn Randolph on as a guest tomorrow?"

"How could I miss it? What harm could it do?"

"Robin, surely you don't think it's a good idea to start promoting our own staff like that!"

Robin made a face. "You're right that it's technically a conflict of interest, since he's a feature on your own show. But the Traveling Man is a separate segment, so..."

"It's still the station's own staff."

"Don't be so stiff-necked, Emily. You're not in journalism school anymore. The rules are different in the real world."

"Ethics are still ethics."

"Well, at least Quinn will be interesting, which is more than you can say about most of the guests Gary brings on the show."

"If he can actually talk without a script," Emily muttered.

Robin laughed. "Don't worry. Gary will take care of that, I'm..." She paused, looked over Emily's shoulder and said under her breath, "Well, I should've known you wouldn't be lucky enough that he'd be somewhere out in western Nebraska today, miles from a television set."

"What do you mean?" Emily twisted around.

In the commissary door, standing quietly and looking over the crowd as if he was searching for someone, was Quinn Randolph.

Emily swallowed hard.

She'd met him before, of course; the station manager had introduced them on Emily's first day on the job. But she had been so tense and excited about everything then that she hadn't paid particular attention, and in the three months since, she hadn't run into him again. If Quinn wasn't traveling the Midwest in that ridiculous recreational vehicle, sending his stories back to the station by microwave relay, he was working a completely different schedule than Emily's early-morning hours.

He looked taller in person. Of course he would, she told herself wildly. She was used to seeing him on a nineteen-inch monitor! But there were other differences, too; his skin had a deeper brown tone, and he wasn't smiling. And his eyes, when his gaze came to rest on her, did not hold the mischie-

vous gleam she was used to seeing in his lighthearted stories. Instead, there was a question, and a glint of
determination, as he started toward her.

She sank back into her chair and shot a look at Robin.
"He doesn't look very happy. Why on earth—"

"Oh, didn't I tell you?" Robin murmured. "Remember
when you made your crack about secretaries and accountants and equal time and finding guests who matter? Well,
your microphone was still live."

Emily's eyes widened in shock. "That went out on the
air?"

"No—just to the control room, and from there to all the
monitors in the station."

And obviously Quinn Randolph had been somewhere in
the building. No wonder he didn't look happy.

Emily could almost feel a chill as he came to stand beside
her—as if she was out in the open and his body was suddenly blocking the sun.

"Have you two met?" Robin asked brightly.

"Oh, we don't need an introduction," Quinn said. "You
don't mind if I join you?" He didn't wait for an answer. He
pulled a chair around and straddled it, propping his arms
across the back so he could rest his chin on his hands and
study Emily.

She sipped her sparkling water and tried not to look at
him.

"What's wrong with having me as a guest?" he asked
gently.

"I didn't object." Why was her voice doing funny things?
She sounded as if her vocal cords needed lubrication. "Not
at all."

Quinn shook his head sadly. "That's not the way I heard
it. You were throwing around high-flying phrases like 'conflict of interest' and—"

"Well, it is," Emily said stubbornly. "That's what I was complaining about. It wasn't anything personal."

His eyelashes really were annoyingly long and black, and curly, too—a complete waste on a man.

"I suppose that should be a comfort," Quinn said lazily. "You know, I never before thought of 'Kansas City Morning' as serious journalism."

"I never said it was, but that doesn't mean we don't pay attention to ethical—"

"In short, it's the usual morning-TV fluff."

The dismissing tone stung Emily's pride. "Kansas City Morning" had its flaws; she wasn't going to defend its every idiosyncrasy. But it was a whole lot better than the average show, and someday it was going to be great. For Quinn to write it off like that, as something of no importance whatsoever, was more than she would sit still for.

"Of course, you're the expert when it comes to fluff," she murmured. She heard Robin suck in her breath in shock.

Quinn didn't turn a hair.

"As a matter of fact, Quinn," Emily added sweetly, "I think you're very good at what you do."

"Thank you." Was it her imagination, or did he sound cautious?

"Showing only your best side to the camera takes practice, I'm sure. And of course if it sometimes requires twelve takes to get it right..."

Quinn started to smile.

The grin and the corresponding sparkle in those clear dark hazel eyes made Emily just a little nervous. "You're lucky to have that luxury. Live television, on the other hand—"

"Simply going on the air live doesn't earn you any points, Emily. But let's go back to the real question—why you feel it's such a threat to the integrity of 'Kansas City Morning' to let me inside your hallowed Studio B."

"I told you it's nothing personal. I just want some ethical standards set, because the show isn't always going to be what it is at the moment."

His eyes narrowed. "I believe I feel the winds of change at 'Kansas City Morning'... Tell me, do you plan to turn it into some kind of investigative-reporting show?"

"Of course not." She stood up. "If you'll excuse me, I think we've taken this discussion as far as—"

Across the room, a chair skidded on the terrazzo floor. Emily spun around just as the earsplitting squeal gave way to a dull thud.

Beside the farthest table, the station manager and the producer of "Kansas City Morning" were leaning over a fallen body. Gary Bennington's.

From the confused babble of voices, she managed to pick out Jason Manning's breathless explanation. "He started to stand up. Then he clutched at his chest and grabbed for the chair—and fell. Call an ambulance, fast!"

Emily was stunned, as incapable of moving as if someone had glued her feet to the floor.

Quinn brushed past her toward the little group clustered around Gary. "Cheer up, Emily," he said over his shoulder. "You may have just gotten your big chance."

BY NOON THERE HAD BEEN no word, and it took every bit of determination Emily possessed to smile and banter her way through her public appearance at the luncheon meeting of a local club. The chicken salad seemed to stick in her throat, and the business discussion went on forever. When it was her turn to say a few words, her speech seemed dull and dry and brittle. With relief, she finally escaped the club members and drove back to the station.

The mood in the building was still somber, and the moment she came in the receptionist at the front door said, "The station manager wants to see you right away, Miss Lambert."

All she could think was, He's going to tell me that Gary's dead. Then Quinn's words echoed in her mind. *You may have just gotten your big chance.*

She tried to swallow the lump in her throat. Damn Quinn Randolph, anyway! How dare he imply she would be happy because of Gary's sudden illness? That had been the farthest thing from her mind.

Yes, she had spent a good part of the past three months planning and daydreaming about how things would be when Gary was gone. Yes, she had looked forward to the time when she would have her own chance to mold and change "Kansas City Morning."

But she hadn't wanted it to come this way.

Jason Manning was waiting for her, as well as the station manager, John Bates. Both of them rose when she came in; Jason, awkwardly solicitous, drew a chair forward for her.

"How's Gary?" she asked.

He shook his head. "He doesn't look good at the moment. It's his heart, of course, and we anticipate he'll be incapacitated for several weeks at least. It will be a few days before the doctors can even say how bad it is and how long he'll be laid up—or if he'll ever be able to return to work."

The pressure in Emily's chest eased a little. At least Gary was still alive; that was a relief. "I'll do the best I can to fill the gap," she said quietly. "No matter what it takes."

"Well, that's really what we wanted to talk to you about, Emily." John leaned forward and steepled his fingers. "It's too bad, happening this way, before you've had a chance to establish yourself."

The tone of his voice sent an icicle down Emily's spine. He sounded sad—the way a boss might just before he fired an employee. But he couldn't dismiss her, could he? It was Jason Manning who'd hired her.

"I've had three months' experience," she began. "I know the ropes, and—"

"Of course you do," Jason said. "And we're counting on you now for some continuity in the show. But we can't possibly expect you to fill your own shoes and Gary's, too. However, under the circumstances, until we know whether he's going to be able to come back, we don't feel we can bring in someone completely new, either."

Emily's head was swimming.

Jason patted her shoulder. "Fortunately, John has come up with the answer—someone who can take Gary's place for whatever length of time he's needed, someone who is already familiar to the viewers and who can easily step into Gary's shoes as host. He'll be great. We're sure you'll agree."

The pressure in Emily's chest, almost a crushing force, had returned. So they were naming a host—not a cohost. They were bringing someone new into her show, over her head.

"He'll need some help learning the ropes, of course, but I know you'll give him a hand."

"Who?" Emily said. Her voice didn't sound familiar.

"Quinn." Jason Manning smiled. "Quinn Randolph. Now I ask you, Emily, isn't that the perfect choice?"

CHAPTER TWO

EMILY DIDN'T EVEN KNOW what she said after that. Obviously she hadn't voiced the things she was thinking, or she wouldn't have left the station manager's office a few minutes later with not only John's heartfelt thanks but Jason Manning's, as well, still ringing in her ears.

She went straight to her dressing room, locked the door and sagged into the armchair.

She could understand why they felt that a show that had always had two hosts could not go on for an indefinite period with only one. As long as there were two experienced hosts on the staff, almost anyone at the station could fill in if one of them needed a day off, because the remaining regular could carry the weight of the show. But if there was only Emily to begin with, and she got a sudden case of laryngitis...

It made perfect sense to fill Gary's shoes; Emily had no quarrel with that. But Quinn Randolph wasn't filling in. He was taking over.

For three months, she had cheerfully played second banana to the star. That had been fine with her; she respected Gary Bennington and the niche he had built for himself, and she expected to have to earn her own place. It took time to learn the system, to be comfortable with the schedule and the cues and the style of the show. She had been willing to stay in the background while she served her apprenticeship. And she knew very well that Gary thought of her in much the same way as he regarded the furniture on the set . . . she was a necessary part of the business, but he would shed no tears if she failed and had to be replaced.

She had no problem accepting those conditions, because she had known from the moment Jason Manning had offered her the job that someday she would be much more. Someday she would occupy the host's chair, and she could begin to restructure "Kansas City Morning" as her own show.

Now she was being displaced by a guy who worked in sound bites. Quinn's longest appearance on the air was his daily ten-minute spot between the evening news and the late-night movie—and that was simply a longer version of whatever story he'd done earlier on "Kansas City Morning." He was a videotape jockey who probably hadn't done two hours of continuous live television in his whole career, much less on a daily basis.

The producer and the station manager had cited Quinn's experience as their reason for choosing him and promoting him over Emily's head. But the fact remained that his experience had nothing at all in common with this new assignment. Emily was the one with experience—but she had been passed by.

She sighed and pushed herself up out of the chair. There was no sense in letting herself drown in a puddle of self-pity. The decision had been made, and there was nothing for her to do but accept it.

She pulled her dressing-room door shut with a bang. With any luck, she mused, Quinn would botch up so badly tomorrow that Jason would relieve him on the spot.

She smiled a little. It was something to dream about, anyway.

As she passed the newsroom, a tall, dark-haired young man came out in a hurry, and Emily, still thinking fondly of the many ways Quinn might mess up, ran headlong into him. He caught her, and Emily held on to his arm while she tried to get her breath back. "Sorry," she gasped, looking up at the perfect classical profile of the station's main news anchor, Brad Jarrett. "I suppose you're on the way to a big story?"

"Not today. Things have been pretty dull. Hey, I'm sorry to hear about Gary."

Emily nodded. "It was a shock. I understand he's doing—"

Brad interrupted. "Wish I'd been there. It would have made great news footage—rescue in progress, CPR and the whole thing. And since it's such a slow news day we've got a hole for it on the six-o'clock broadcast, too." He shook his head with regret. "It could have been a prizewinner. Too bad nobody thought to grab a camera."

Emily stared at him. The man was obviously serious; Gary's collapse was no more to him than an award-winning way to demonstrate cardiopulmonary resuscitation. "Sorry, Brad, but it never occurred to me," she said crisply.

"Well, no use crying over spilled milk, I suppose. Who's going to take his place, do you know?"

There wasn't any sense in avoiding the question, Emily thought. The news had probably hit the station grapevine already. "Quinn Randolph's going to fill in for a while."

"Till Jason finds a permanent replacement?"

Emily looked up at Brad. "I don't think you should jump to the conclusion that Jason's looking for a replacement."

Brad's elegantly curved eyebrows drew together in thought. "You don't mean they'd leave Quinn in that job forever. He's all right in a pinch, I guess, but he's hardly the kind to light fires at the viewers' breakfast tables."

"I mean that it's quite likely Gary will make a full recovery."

"Oh, come on. How old is Gary—sixty? Even if he does get well—which, let's face it, is doubtful—he won't be back. It's a great excuse for Jason to ease Gary out of his little fiefdom and get someone in there who can really do the job."

Emily was feeling slightly ill at the whole line of reasoning. "Let's not bury him till he's dead, all right?" she snapped, and started off toward the main door.

"Hey, I was only telling you what I see," Brad called after her.

Emily didn't bother to answer.

At the hospital, an aide greeted her at the formidable doors of the intensive-care unit. She shook her head when Emily asked to see Gary. "Only family members can go into the unit," she said, "and then only for five minutes out of each hour."

Emily couldn't argue with that. "I'd like him to know I came, at least."

"Oh, I'll tell him. What's the name? You look awfully familiar...." The aide snapped her fingers. "I know. You're Emily, aren't you? I watch you whenever I can. My shifts change, so sometimes I have to miss." She seized Emily's hand and shook it. "You can write Mr. Bennington a note if you like. I'll give it to him myself." She pulled a notepad out of her pocket and handed it over. "Wait till I tell my girlfriends I actually met you!"

"Thanks." Emily scribbled a two-line message and handed the notepad back. "You're likely to get a flood of cards and flowers, you know," she warned, "as soon as his audience realizes he's ill."

The aide looked concerned. "He can't have flowers as long as he's in the unit. Or fruit baskets, either. But mail's all right, as long as there's not too much."

"Well, brace yourself for bags of it. As soon as I tell the viewers tomorrow morning that he's here..."

It hadn't occurred to her until just then that someone was going to have to tell the viewers, and she thought it over as she left the hospital. Just how was she going to phrase the announcement? The rule was to always tell the truth, but underplay the severity of the situation. In a case like this, however, when the truth didn't look terribly reassuring....

"Maybe I should just leave it to Quinn," she muttered. "If he's going to be host, he'll have to learn to deal with crises like this. And if he doesn't do it well..."

TUESDAY MORNING WAS COLD, crisp and clear, and the sunrise was spectacular, a symphony of pink and purple and gold. Emily didn't stand around outside to admire it, though, because she could see her breath as she walked from her car to the station's main door. The calendar said spring had arrived the week before, but the chill in the air told a different story.

She was not alone; a car had pulled in right before hers. When she came up to the station, Quinn was waiting by the door. He was little more than a dark shadow, in a black turtleneck and jeans and a denim jacket. He unlocked the door and held it for her without a word.

"No recreational vehicle this morning?" She turned toward her dressing room.

He dropped into step beside her. "I'm not attached to it with a lifeline. And to answer your question from yesterday, I don't live in it, either, except when I'm on the road with a camera crew and we have to."

Emily's eyebrows rose a fraction. "You sound a bit irritable this morning, Quinn. What's wrong? Now that you've got this wonderful opportunity to showcase your talents..."

"You think this job was my idea?" he growled. "Any occupation that requires getting up at four in the morning isn't at the top of my list of desirable professions."

"Ah," Emily murmured, "that explains it. You had a hot date last night and didn't want to call it off."

One corner of his mouth turned up a bit. "As a matter of fact, I was in bed by ten."

Emily stopped at her dressing-room door and smiled sweetly up at him. "And you expect me to ask whose bed it was? If you think I'm going to get tangled up in that line, Quinn, you're incredibly naive."

He leaned lazily against the wall and studied her. The dark hazel gaze obviously didn't miss a detail, from her faded jeans and running shoes to the still-damp hair, caught in a careless knot at the nape of her neck. "You don't look precisely sunny this morning yourself. What's your excuse?"

Emily put her chin up a fraction and ignored the question. "If you don't mind, Quinn, I'd like to make the announcement about Gary."

He shrugged. "If you want." He pushed himself away from the wall. "See you on the set at seven." He strolled off down the hall.

"Seven?" Emily called after him. "That's airtime. Don't you think we should make it fifteen minutes early so we can get things straight? At least run through the opening?"

Quinn turned around, hooked his thumbs in the pockets of his jeans and shook his head disapprovingly. "I'm disappointed in you, Emily. The champion of live TV, wanting a rehearsal? After three months, I'd think openings and closings would be so automatic you could do them in your sleep." He frowned a little. "Come to think of it, that might be an improvement."

Emily slammed her dressing-room door. The sound reverberated down the hallway—but so did Quinn's chuckle, and she didn't feel as if she'd made much of a point, after all.

He was as good as his word; he appeared on the set of Studio B at precisely one minute to seven. The jeans and turtleneck had given way to a very nice brown tweed sports jacket, dark brown trousers, a cream-colored shirt and an absolutely proper, subtly striped tie. He paused at the edge of the set for a moment, looking it over with an expression Emily would swear was caution. Then he slowly stepped onto the elevated stage and sat down on the love seat next to her.

Emily shifted nervously. Gary had always occupied the club chair beside the fake fireplace, so she had never noticed before that the love seat wasn't really big enough for two people. She could actually feel the heat of Quinn's body.

"Um... Quinn," she began. "Could you—"

"Stand by," the director warned from the door of the control room.

Emily sighed and sat up very straight. From the corner of her eye she could see the monitor. The center panel was showing the opening credits, and the theme music played softly in the background. "'Kansas City Morning,'" the voice-over said, "with Gary Bennington and Emily Lambert..."

She focused her eyes on the teleprompter just above the camera lens. She tried not to rely on it. Reading the screen was a bad habit, because one tended not to think about the words, and that led to all kinds of complications. Still, it was nice to have a crutch handy on occasions like this when one's mind went completely blank....

As the camera's red light blinked on, she smiled and said, "Welcome to 'Kansas City Morning.' I'm Emily—"

"I should hope you're not Gary," the man beside her said easily.

She tossed him a smile that threatened less-pleasant action if he followed up the remark. "And Quinn Randolph is sitting in for Gary today. Gary suffered some chest pain yesterday, and is hospitalized while the doctors check him over. We hope he'll be back very soon." She glanced at Quinn to see his reaction to the extra meaning in that last phrase.

She had seen him smile a hundred times over the past few months, but that had been on videotape, on the monitor. Seeing Quinn Randolph's smile life-size and close up was a different thing altogether.

It started with a sparkle in his eyes. Then one corner of his mouth slowly quirked upward, and white teeth gleamed. She realized that her fingertips were actually tingling with the desire to smooth out the crinkle of laugh lines at the corners of his eyes. She clasped her hands together, hard, in her lap.

"Emily," he mused, "you sound as if you don't like my company. What can I do to make you feel better about being stuck with me?" His eyes were full of concern, but he didn't wait for an answer.

That was wise of him, Emily thought. Not that she *had* an answer; that smile seemed to have knocked out her power of speech. It was deadly at close range—a thousand volts of energy that threatened to interfere with the power supply in the whole studio, to say nothing of disabling the cohost.

Quinn turned businesslike. "We have several fascinating guests for you this morning, including the author of a new bestseller set in Kansas City. But first, an update on the news from Brad Jarrett."

Emily blinked in surprise. Brad was in the newsroom at this hour? He usually left the daytime anchor slots to the junior staff members and didn't turn up himself till midafternoon, when it was time to start assembling the widely viewed evening news. Not that it mattered why he was in the station, of course; Emily had more important things to think about.

"I'll do the author interview," she told Quinn during the break. "I've read the book. You can handle the beauty pageant winner, can't you? Just ask a couple of questions about the contest. That's all you'll have time for, anyway. Then in the next hour—"

"I think I can manage to muddle through," Quinn murmured. "I've noticed that you always look a bit scared on the air, as if Gary might snap at you."

"I do not!"

"But do you realize he's got you running in circles even when he isn't here?"

Emily took a deep breath and counted to ten. "I want the show to go smoothly. Is there anything wrong with that?"

"Not exactly. But what could it hurt to relax a little?"

"Fine. I'll relax. And if you fall on your face, it's not my problem."

"Ah, now I begin to understand what Jason saw in you." The note of satisfaction in Quinn's voice made Emily want to hit him. "There is a little fire deep inside you, after all. You're not just another one of Gary's plastic dolls."

He turned back to the camera as the red light blinked on. "Thanks, Brad. You know, Emily, we're short a guest this morning—since I was supposed to be it."

"If you'd rather change hats, Quinn . . ."

"Oh, no. I'm enjoying myself just the way things are. But as long as we have some time to chat, let's discuss you." He leaned back. Emily thought she saw a flicker of discomfort in his eyes as his spine hit the hard cushions of the love seat. "In the three months since you came to 'Kansas City Morning,' you really haven't told the viewers much about Emily Lambert. I'm curious."

"You just haven't been watching, Quinn."

"Of course I've been watching." The statement was ordinary enough; it was the inflection of his voice that turned it into flirtation. "So last night, after I was asked to join you today, I did my research."

Emily watched with foreboding as he tugged a folded sheet of paper from the inside breast pocket of his jacket and spread it out on his knee with incredible care. "What have you got there?"

"I went to the library—" Quinn let his voice drop to a conspiratorial whisper "—and I found a magazine profile on you that was done two years ago, while you were still in radio."

Emily remembered it. Furthermore, she could see over his shoulder that he had underlined whole passages of type. "That was a silly—"

"But interesting, you must admit. For the sake of your listeners, who of course could only imagine you, the magazine even gave a description."

"Quinn, for the sake of the viewers who don't have that disadvantage—"

"It says, for instance, that your hair is dark brown. I've always thought myself that it was just short of red, but maybe that's because of the television lights. Am I the only one..." He looked around regretfully. "If we just had a studio audience, Emily, we could take a vote. Well, never mind. Let's move on. This says you've got brown velvet eyes..."

Through the glass that separated the control room from the studio, Emily could see the director, her fingertips pressed hard against her temples as if her head was throbbing. Emily didn't doubt that Tish was in agony; she was watching the show go straight down the drain. And Quinn didn't seem to care.

Then the light dawned. Of course—Quinn was *trying* to get himself kicked off the show. That was the only explanation. He hadn't been joking about his objections to getting up at four in the morning; he really didn't want this job.

All right, Emily decided. If Quinn wanted to hang himself, why shouldn't she help by playing out a little rope now and then?

He was peering thoughtfully into her eyes. "Brown velvet," he repeated thoughtfully. "Well, I'll have to think about that."

Emily did her best not to giggle. "One of my boyfriends wrote a poem about them once," she volunteered. "But it wasn't a very good poem, I'm afraid."

"I think I could get to like this job," Quinn said with satisfaction. He looked at the story again. "Is it true, for instance, that you got so many love letters from your listeners the radio station had a special recycling bin set aside for them?"

"Why do you want to know?" she asked innocently. "Because you lack ideas of your own? If I'd realized you needed help with your love life, Quinn, I'd have kept every one."

Quinn's eyebrows arched a little. "Honey, I have no trouble being original. Oh, I see it's time for the weather, and here's the first Robin of spring to tell us about it."

The monitor cut to Robin in the weather room, and Emily relaxed as best she could against the hard love seat and smiled. This wasn't going to be so difficult after all. "I'm on to you, Quinn Randolph."

"Are you now?" Quinn murmured. "That should make life a little more dangerous."

Emily couldn't remember a show ever going by so fast. Before she'd drawn a full breath, it seemed, Quinn was politely prompting her to say goodbye. "I know it's tough to think of leaving me," he said earnestly, "but remember—it's only till tomorrow." Then his eyes brightened. "Unless you'd like—"

"I don't think so."

"But you didn't even let me ask!"

"Save it for tomorrow, Quinn. Goodbye, everybody!" She gave her special wave, a sign-language symbol that formed a shorthand message for Gran, and the closing credits began to roll.

Within seconds, the director was on the set, screaming, "Quinn, don't you ever watch the control room? I had to cancel two guests because you didn't leave time for them!"

Quinn looked stricken. "Tish, that's terrible! Are they still here so I can tell them how sorry I am? It's my inexperience, you know. Do you think they'll come again another time?"

Emily bit her lip, hard, to keep from grinning.

Tish shook her fist at him. "You ignored the damned cues, Quinn!"

"Cues?" he said innocently. "I saw you waving your arms around—is that what you were trying to tell me? Well, I'll just have to learn. In the meantime, you might cancel half of tomorrow's guests, too, so we can really enjoy the ones we keep." He stepped down off the stage. "I'll be in the greenroom apologizing for the feelings I hurt if you need me."

Emily put her hand over her mouth.

Tish turned to her, eyes wild. "How could you let him get away with that?"

Emily was astounded. "Me? What was *I* supposed to do? Kick him in the kneecap? You had control of his microphone, at least. You could have turned him into a mime!"

Quinn said over his shoulder, "Traitor. Don't give her ideas."

"What's Gary going to say?" Tish moaned.

Emily gathered up her notes. It had been a waste of time to write them out; she hadn't used a single one. "Think positive," she recommended. "His doctor won't allow visitors, so maybe he had the good sense to eliminate television, too. And if Gary didn't see that fiasco for himself, Tish, you don't want to tell him about it."

Once back in her tiny dressing room, Emily figured she was safe for a little while. But before she had managed to change clothes there were two separate knocks on the door. The first was Robin, warning her that, even before the show was over, the station switchboard had lighted up like New York harbor on the Fourth of July.

Emily groaned. The message was clear. A woman of discretion would make herself scarce until the fireworks were over and the dust had settled. Of course, her motive wasn't only to avoid trouble. Obviously she'd never get any work done in this zoolike atmosphere; she'd better go home where she could concentrate.

Still in her slip, she was starting to load up her backpack when the second knock sounded. "You can't come in," she called.

"I don't want to," Quinn answered. "I want you to come out and go to breakfast with me. We can talk about how to run the show tomorrow."

Emily wrapped a robe around herself and opened the door two inches. "No. In the first place, I have a public appearance at noon today, so I don't have time for breakfast."

Quinn looked at his watch and started to speak.

Emily went on, "In the second place, this morning you left the distinct impression that you didn't want to schedule things. And in the third place, don't you think we should wait to see if there's going to *be* a tomorrow?" She shut the door in his face.

A mournful voice from the hallway said, "I didn't think you were the kind to kick a man when he's down."

Emily felt a momentary twinge, then told herself firmly that any trouble Quinn Randolph faced was certainly of his own making. If he intended to turn tomorrow's show into even more of a circus—assuming Jason Manning hadn't fired him by then—she didn't want to know about it ahead of time.

He was nowhere in sight twenty minutes later when she finished changing into a fresh dress for her noon appearance. With her backpack slung over her shoulder, she headed for the main door.

The receptionist at the front desk looked frazzled. "The producer of that show is Mr. Manning," she was saying as Emily came within hearing distance. "He's on another line. If you'll hold, I'll connect you as soon as he's free." Her voice had a worn edge, as if she'd said the same thing a hundred times already. Emily thought she probably had.

The receptionist cupped her hand over the telephone and ignored the five blinking lights on the console in front of her. "Mr. Manning's secretary wants you right away."

"Thanks. I'm awfully sorry about the telephones."

A strained smile was her only answer; the receptionist had already punched into the next call.

In the waiting room just outside Jason Manning's office, Tish was lounging in a deep leather chair. Her posture was careless, but Emily could tell from the way she clutched her coffee cup that the director expected the sky to fall at any moment.

"You wanted me?" Emily asked the secretary, expecting to be told to take a seat next to Tish and join her vigil.

But the secretary handed her a videotape. "It's a movie preview that just arrived. The star is one of the guests tomorrow."

Tish said under her breath, "Always assuming that Quinn doesn't keep him waiting till he blows up and walks out."

Emily found a spot in her bag for the tape. "After this morning? Surely the Traveling Man will be told to hit the road."

Tish set her cup down with a thump. "I don't know. The one thing I've learned in this business is that you can never predict what crazy notion a producer will get into his head. He might just decide that no amount of angry callers will tell him how to run his show."

Tish was right about that, Emily thought. Jason Manning might not back down so abruptly, after all.

She ducked out of the station as quickly as she could. Right now, she needed an island of sanity.

In the house in Brookside, Carrie Lambert was sitting in her low, armless rocking chair in the big front parlor. Around her on the carpet lay yards of white tulle so fine and sheer the fabric looked almost like a cloud. Her hands, small and wrinkled, moved surely over the edge of the bridal veil, attaching infinitesimal beads in what looked like a random pattern.

Emily edged close enough to kiss Gran's cheek and then backed cautiously away from the drifting fabric.

Carrie's hands didn't stop as she looked speculatively up at Emily. "What are you doing home at this hour?"

"I have a few minutes to kill before I have to turn up at the flower show to present the prizes."

"And you wanted to get out of the studio before the roof caved in?"

"Something like that. Was it so obvious on the air?"

"I thought the TV was going to explode."

Emily sighed. "I was afraid of that. Sometimes radio was easier." She sank down on a footstool and absentmindedly fingered the beaded edge of the veil. "No cohosts, no levels of bureaucracy, no real rules. I could be as outrageous as I wanted, and nobody seemed to care."

"That's because the station manager had too many other things on his mind to worry about what you were doing. Also, you had a much smaller audience."

"Thanks, Gran. Rub it in, why don't you?"

Carrie shrugged. "I'm just telling the truth. Are you sorry you made the change?"

Sorry to leave a tiny radio station that hardly covered a single county—Gran was right about the size of the audience—for an independent television station known throughout the Midwest? Sorry to give up her job as radio jack-of-all-trades for a high-profile position on "Kansas City Morning"? True, at the radio station she'd had her own talk show, but there had never been much opportunity to make something more of herself; when the show wasn't on the air, she'd filled in wherever she was needed—twelve-hour days with little chance of advancement. It had been sheer good luck when Jason Manning had tuned into her show and liked her style enough to seek her out.

Emily shook her head. "No, Gran, I'm not sorry."

"In that case, you have to make the best of the situation. It'll straighten itself out." Carrie pointed to a foam mannequin head that stood on a nearby table. "Try on that headpiece for me, will you? The bride's coming for a fitting tomorrow, and I don't want to get a shock when she puts it on."

Emily eyed the satin confection perching so precariously on the foam that it had to be pinned in place. "I can understand why you're doubtful. Is it supposed to be only half a hat?"

Carrie shrugged. "That's what she said she wanted."

The headpiece cupped the right side of Emily's head; a cluster of tiny satin-ribbon roses swirled down over her ear and brushed her cheek. But the other half of her head was left bare. She looked at herself in the long mirror mounted on one of the pocket doors between the twin parlors. "I don't know, Gran. It's awfully strange. How are you going to attach the veil so the weight of it doesn't drag the headpiece off?"

Carrie reached up and spread her fingertips across Emily's hair at the edge of the headpiece. "Right here. It's supposed to sort of swirl down and around her body."

"Well, that's a relief. I thought maybe it was just going to trail over her right shoulder and leave the other one bare—as if she couldn't make up her mind about whether to wear a veil at all. What does this woman look like?" She lifted off the headpiece. The comb that had anchored it to the top of her head caught in her hair and pulled her chignon loose. "Darn it, and Joanie worked so hard on this, too." She glanced at her watch and started pulling out hairpins. "Well, I can't take time to fuss with it or I'll be late. I'll see you this afternoon, Gran."

At every red light between Brookside and Overland Park she picked up her hairbrush, and by the time she reached the shopping mall where the flower show was being held, her hair was shining and bouncy, free of the heavy spray Joanie had used for the show that morning.

Emily felt free in other ways, too. She was glad she had stopped to talk to her grandmother; now she had things back in perspective. It was amazing how comforting Gran could be. And she was right—the situation would sort itself out.

In the section of the mall that had been roped off for the luncheon and awards, Emily was immediately surrounded and assaulted with questions about Gary's health and what was going to happen to "Kansas City Morning." "Gary will be fine, I'm sure," she answered as soon she could make herself heard, and crossed her fingers behind her back. "I'm sorry he couldn't be here with me today to help with the prizes as you'd planned, but I'll do my best. And as for the program—"

Behind her, Quinn said, "Don't waste your breath. I told them it's just a temporary change, but they didn't seem convinced."

Emily wheeled around. "What are you doing here?"

He shrugged. "Jason's secretary sent me. She said Gary was supposed to be here, so I might as well fill in." He reached for her hand and tucked it cozily into the bend of his elbow. "So, Emily dear, where do I start filling?"

CHAPTER THREE

QUINN WAS AN ENGAGING sort, Emily had to give him that. The man could have charmed a swath through a hostile army, so the flower-club ladies who'd had their hearts set on meeting Gary Bennington were no challenge at all. Even the woman at the head table who was irate because her carefully lettered place cards were no longer accurate warmed up to him eventually; and she was forced to admit that Gary's absence wasn't Quinn's fault.

At the luncheon, he was seated on one side of the club president; Emily was on the other. The head table was elevated a little, and at their backs was a massive planting of lush tropical ferns and palms, a permanent feature of the mall decor. The rest of the luncheon tables were set at oblique angles so everyone had a good view of the special guests, and surrounding the entire area were long racks full of flowers. Emily had never seen so many elaborate arrangements in one place.

When the president excused herself for a moment to deal with some club business, Emily took advantage of the opportunity to sneak a glance at Quinn. He was listening with every sign of fascination to the place-card lady, but he was poking at his salad and looking doubtfully at a yellow-orange blossom that lay atop the neat pile of lettuce.

She leaned across the president's chair and hissed, "It's edible."

"You're sure it's not in there by accident?"

The president returned just then, and Emily couldn't see whether Quinn took her word for it and ate the nasturtium blossom or simply pushed it aside.

"It's such a treat for us to have you come, Emily," the president said. "Especially under the circumstances."

"Oh, I wouldn't dream of standing you up just because Gary's ill."

"That's not what I meant. Having you and Quinn here on your first day together is an incredible feather in the garden club's hat, you know."

And possibly, Emily thought, it's our *last* day together, too. That would make the occasion even more special. "You watched the show this morning?"

"Oh, yes. It was the most astounding thing I've seen in months. Phenomenal, in fact."

Emily couldn't decide if the woman was telling the truth or only being polite. Perhaps she really had enjoyed the fireworks. On the other hand, proper manners dictated that she wouldn't tell a guest she'd hated the performance. And she hadn't precisely said she'd liked the show; "astounding" and "phenomenal" could have lots of meanings.

The president said a good many flattering things while she was introducing them. Emily, however, wasn't listening; she was studying the single microphone, attached to the podium with a short flexible rod, and thinking that she'd give a great deal right now for a wireless like the ones they used in the studio. A single stationary microphone was a nuisance. For both of them to use it, they'd practically have to be hugging!

To make matters worse, Quinn immediately adjusted the microphone to a good six inches higher than Emily would have liked it.

"If you want to do all the work," Emily pointed out, "that's fine with me."

He moved the microphone down and grinned at her. "I was just waiting to see how long it would take you to complain. I'll bet you couldn't keep your mouth shut for ten minutes even if it was sealed with duct tape."

"Of course not, if you're talking, because you can't go ten minutes without needing a correction."

Appreciative laughter rippled across the audience. Emily was startled; she'd thought the welcoming applause, coupled with the badly placed microphone, would make her inaudible.

Quinn turned his smile on the crowd. "I didn't have any warning about this, you understand." The intimate tone of his voice made his words seem like a secret confidence. "They only told me at the station this morning that I was judging a flower show, and frankly, I panicked. I know a rose when I buy one, but—"

"Isn't he *talented?*" Emily interrupted. "Of course, he's no doubt bought quite a few of them—over the years."

"It hasn't been *that* many years," Quinn objected. "I could also probably name a violet if it hit me in the face. But as for recognizing the skill and dedication I'm sure goes into growing and arranging these flowers, no. I'd probably give the prize to a bunch of dandelions."

"Good thing you're not judging, then."

"When I found out that all I had to do was eat lunch and hand out the prizes and kiss the winners, I said, hey, I'm your man."

"Especially when it comes to kissing the winners," Emily put in.

"But I do have one personal award to offer. The first-place prize for hot and peppery goes to whatever those flowers in the salad were."

"Nasturtiums," Emily volunteered.

Quinn looked at her inquiringly for an instant, and then his brow cleared. "Gesundheit, dear."

There was another wave of laughter and some scattered applause.

"That was not at all how I'd expect a pretty little flower to taste. But then I've known a few people who are that way, too—innocent and inviting on the outside but quite a surprise package when you get closer." He glanced at Emily. "Not that I'm giving names, you understand. Now for the prizes..."

By the time the last prizewinner was kissed, there was no doubt that Quinn was the hit of the day. And Emily was basking in the glow of audience approval, too; every time she stepped in to correct one of Quinn's outrageous statements, the laughter had grown stronger. After the last trophy was awarded and the program closed, they were surrounded by club members who had questions or wanted autographs.

Quinn signed a program with a flourish and looked over at Emily. "We do so much better with an appreciative audience," he mused. "We really ought to ask all these folks to come down to the station and help us out tomorrow morning, too."

An elderly woman shook Emily's hand and thanked her for coming, adding, "You're such a lucky woman, you know. You're lovely and warm and charming—and you've got *him*." She tipped her head toward Quinn.

"I don't—" Emily began, but someone else thrust an autograph book at her, and by the time she'd signed it the elderly woman was gone. Not that it mattered, she supposed. Public perception was such a funny thing; if the woman wanted to believe that the byplay she'd watched was something more than an act, Emily's protests wouldn't convince her otherwise.

The president came over to thank them and asked, "Now that you're occupied with 'Kansas City Morning,' Quinn, what are you going to do about your own show?"

"For the present, the Traveling Man will stay close to Kansas City. For instance—" he raised his voice a little "—I've been thinking for some time about doing a piece on the best sweet roll in the metropolitan area, so if any of you are gourmet bakers, too, and want to send me samples now that the flower show isn't taking up all your time..." He took Emily's arm. "Let's go, my dear. The first rule of show business is always to leave them begging for more." He waved happily at the crowd and swept her off down the mall.

"You sounded like the one who was begging," Emily pointed out. "Honestly, Quinn. Cadging handouts like that!"

"Well, finding the best sweet roll is important research, and somebody's got to do it."

Emily let it pass and tried to pull away from him. "We've missed the entrance."

Quinn tucked her hand tighter into the crook of his arm. "I saw something up here I want you to look at. Would you rather I didn't do the sweet-roll story?"

"Why do you care what I think?"

"Well, if you'd like, we could go on location together."

The words held a sultry suggestiveness that made Emily look up at him with suspicion, but his tone was purely businesslike and his eyes held only friendly interest.

"We could do 'Kansas City Morning' from the RV, too, from almost anywhere. That's the beauty of microwave relays."

"If we're in Columbia or Branson, we could hardly call the show 'Kansas City Morning.'"

"That would be a problem," Quinn admitted. "Of course, we could just change the name. Let's see..."

Emily wasn't about to get dragged into that discussion. "The only good thing I can see about the whole plan," she said, "is that if you and I and Tish and the entire crew are out in the RV when Gary sees a television set, he can't call us."

"Now you're thinking!" Quinn stopped in front of a boutique.

Emily followed his gaze to the window display of a mannequin in a long, slinky off-white linen skirt. The buttons that fastened it down the side ended well above the knee, leaving a side slit that could be anything from discreet to daring. "Is that what you wanted me to see? It's a nice skirt, but—"

"You'd look good in it, too."

It was funny, Emily thought, how the simplest compliment could send a warm feeling straight through her.

"You've got much better legs than the average mannequin," Quinn finished. "But as a matter of fact, that wasn't it at all." He guided her toward the furniture shop next door. "There."

In the window stood a pair of tall chairs, gracefully shaped and generously proportioned, with curved dark wood frames and soft beige cushions. "Bar stools?" she said disbelievingly. "Don't tell me you're setting up housekeeping and want my opinion on furniture."

"Not exactly. And they're not bar stools. Come and try them out."

Emily sighed and followed him. He did not offer to help her up into the chair; in fact, when she put out a hand to him to steady herself, Quinn shook his head and stood by with his arms crossed. Still, climbing into the chair wasn't as tough as Emily thought it might be. The foot rail was in exactly the right place to let her cross her legs in her favorite position, and the chair back was firm but comfortable.

"That looked very graceful," Quinn said. "I thought it probably would, but I wanted to be sure." He seized a stand mirror off a nearby table and tipped it so she could see herself. "And check out the nice turn of the ankle. Very elegant."

"Why are you worried about my ankles?"

"Do you have an extra business card with you?"

Emily fumbled in her bag. "I think so. Why?"

"Because the chairs are much better than that low, hard love seat, don't you think?" Quinn turned to the salesclerk and handed him the card. "We'll take four of these. Bill them to Tish Grant, in care of 'Kansas City Morning,' and deliver them to this address."

"I don't know if I..." The salesclerk looked doubtfully at Quinn and then at the card, and turned a wide-eyed gaze on Emily. "Oh, I know you! I watch you every morning."

"Thank you," she said automatically. "That's very nice of you. Quinn, I don't think this is such a good—"

"It's a wonderful idea." He helped her down out of the chair. "That set desperately needs some variety. Two chairs for us, two for guests...it'll change the whole atmosphere."

"Don't you think you should talk to Tish first? And maybe wait a while before you start redecorating the place?"

He shrugged. "My spine won't stand another day on that love seat. Besides, Tish has had years to do this, and she hasn't taken the initiative. She won't, either, because—"

Emily nodded. "—she doesn't have to sit on the furniture. I know. Still, it's my business card that's going to arrive taped to the damned things, Quinn. She'll think I did it."

"Well," Quinn said reasonably, "I don't have my new cards printed yet, and I don't think the salesman would have taken my word about my job change."

"At this rate, you won't need to worry about cards," Emily muttered.

Quinn paused in front of the boutique again. "As long as we're spending money, I'd like to see what the slit in that skirt looks like when you're sitting."

"No," Emily said.

"Is that firm, or can you be persuaded? Where do you get your clothes for the show, anyway?"

"Wardrobe produces them."

"Without asking your opinion?"

"Usually. Why?"

"It's a relief to know the crazy taste isn't yours."

Emily put her chin up a little. "Would you care to define 'crazy'?"

Quinn didn't seem to hear. "I'll bet they've got orders from Gary to keep you toned down."

"Why on earth would Gary want to do any such thing?"

"So you don't get too much attention on camera, of course. I think I'll do a little investigating. And if that's what's been going on—" he started to whistle thoughtfully "—then I'll just take over the job."

Emily bit her tongue. It didn't matter, she told herself. He wasn't going to be part of "Kansas City Morning" long enough to make any lasting impact.

And she was glad.

THERE WAS AN AWFUL LOT of noise around the station the next morning; even in her dressing room Emily could hear the rumblings, and it didn't take a genius to conclude that Tish was on the warpath. Emily just hoped it was only Quinn the director was after. If those chairs had arrived ...

Well, it would be better to talk about it after the show, when the pressure wouldn't be quite so strong on any of them.

Cowardly as it might be, she stayed hidden in her dressing room as long as she could and walked into the studio precisely five minutes before they were to go on the air.

The room was mayhem. On the set, Tish was shaking a fist at Quinn. Quinn was clipping on his wireless mike and reciting a test for the sound technician, apparently ignoring Tish. The usual bustle of cameramen and crew occupied the center of the studio, and in the seats that lined the far wall...

Emily blinked and looked again. Not all the seats were full, but the crowd wouldn't have fit on an average city bus. She recognized a few faces from the flower show; some of the women waved or called her name. But where had the others come from?

She sighed and made her way toward the set. The love seat had been pushed back at an angle, and two of the new stools occupied center stage. As she stepped up on the platform, the technician finished with Quinn and handed Emily a wireless microphone. She clipped the battery to the back of her skirt and fished the tiny mike around her waist to fasten just below the frilly collar of her peach-colored blouse.

Nothing like having an audience while I finish getting decked out, she thought. But there wasn't time to take the thing to her dressing room.

Quinn was saying earnestly, "But now that they're here, what are you going to do about it, Tish? You can't throw them out. Think of the bad public relations it would create for the show."

"You did this deliberately!"

"I didn't plan it, Tish. Honestly."

Maybe he hadn't planned it, Emily thought. But he'd provoked it.

Quinn put his arm around the director's shoulders and urged her off the set. "There's no time, Tish. You can't get them out now."

"Dammit, Quinn..." Tish glanced at the clock above the control-room window. It was one minute to airtime. "All right, have it your own way." She brushed past Emily, muttering, "Give the man an inch, and he thinks he's a ruler."

Quinn put two fingers in his mouth and gave an earsplitting whistle. The noise level in the studio receded. "Sit down, everybody," he ordered. "Remember, you're a test case. It's up to you whether there will ever again be a live audience for this show, so behave yourselves, all right?" He gestured toward the tall chairs. "Good morning, Em."

"Morning," she said dutifully. "I'm not sure it's so good."

The control room signaled, the camera's red light blinked, and she flashed a smile and introduced herself as always.

Quinn did the same. Then he leaned back and gave a satisfied sigh and said, "Don't you think these are nice chairs, Emily?"

"Not bad at all. When Gary comes back maybe we'll find you a job as chief furniture procurer."

His smile flashed. "Oh, if you think I'm good at chairs, wait till you see what I can do with—" he paused "—other furniture."

At least he hadn't come straight out and said "beds." Emily cut in quickly. "I think maybe we'd better move on to the news, don't you, Quinn?"

"When we're having such fun?" He flicked a fingertip against a soft tendril of hair over her ear. "I like the French braid this morning, but it's a shame all the pretty stuff is at the back of your head where nobody can see it."

"Thanks for the compliment, Quinn," she said dryly. "I've been told before that I'm not exactly a beauty, but never that the back of my head is preferable to my face."

"I didn't say that!"

"You certainly did." She looked out at the studio audience. "Didn't he?"

The answer came in a roar that even the tiny directional microphones couldn't miss. "Yes!"

"See?" Emily said, satisfied.

Quinn looked properly chastened. "I only meant that the pretty part of the hairstyle is at the—"

The audience roared again.

Emily slid back in her chair and recrossed her legs. Her skirt crept a little higher; she didn't pay any attention. "I might get to like this idea of yours for a studio audience."

"As long as they're on your side, I'm sure you will." He sighed and raised his hands in a gesture of surrender. "All right, I'm caught in my own web. I apologize. But at least turn around for a minute and let the home audience see for itself."

Emily obligingly swiveled her chair to one side so the camera could focus. "Do you want me to keep my back turned for the rest of the show?" she asked over her shoulder.

"Of course not. Actually I like your hair best of all when it's down around your shoulders, loose and mussed up." Quinn tugged at the silky peach bow securing the end of her long dark braid. "Or wet," he added thoughtfully. "Like right after you get out of the shower and—"

"Quinn!"

"What did I say now? Oh, I know. You want me to make it plain that I wasn't anywhere near the shower while you were in it." His voice held an earnest note, which somehow made the statement even more outrageously unbelievable.

Emily gave up. "The news, Quinn," she reminded him.

"Oh, right. I almost forgot poor Brad, patiently waiting in the newsroom."

With the studio audience watching every move, there wasn't even a chance to relax while the camera was off. Behind the glass wall of the control room, Emily could see Tish pacing like a panther in a cage.

Emily put a fingertip over her microphone, just in case. "Why's Brad here at this hour, anyway?"

Quinn shrugged. "You've got me. Maybe Sir Golden Tongue has been demoted to the day shift."

"I don't think so. He was still doing the late evening news last night. I watched the tape this morning."

His eyebrows rose a fraction. "You're such a Brad Jarrett junkie that you tape him?"

"No, I just think I should keep up on what's happening. It would be pretty embarrassing if California had the big earthquake and I didn't know it when I went on the air the next morning. And I tape the news—or rather the control room does it for me—because I'm always tucked in and snoozing by the time the late broadcast comes on."

"Well, it's a relief to know it's not Brad himself you're hooked on. The only qualification the man has is the ability to say 'toy boat' and other assorted tongue twisters repeatedly and very fast while he's smiling."

Emily bit her lip to keep from laughing.

News gave way to the advertising break, and finally the studio camera went live again. "As long as we're updating the news, Emily, do you have any news on Gary Bennington? How is he this morning?"

"I talked to one of his nurses just a few minutes before we came on the air, and he's doing better, but of course he's still in intensive care."

"Will you be visiting him today?"

Emily suppressed a shudder at the idea. The first thing Gary would ask was how the show was going, and Emily didn't like the choices she would face then. She could lie and assure him that "Kansas City Morning" was doing just fine. Or she could tell the truth and probably propel him into another heart attack.

She shook her head. "He's not receiving visitors yet, except family. He can have cards, though. In fact, we've gotten some already here at the station, and I'll take them over later today."

"Let me know if you need the RV," Quinn suggested.

"And you'll help haul the bags of mail? Thanks, Quinn, I may take you up on that." But not till next week, she thought, or whenever Gary could receive company, so Quinn could help explain the mess they were in!

"Our first guest this morning..." She launched into an introduction of the Hollywood star.

If Gary had been there, of course, this would have been his interview. Emily would have moved off the set during the news break, and the star would have come out, taken his place on the love seat, answered half a dozen questions and gone away to be replaced after an advertising break by yet another guest. The questions would have been good ones, as Gary's always were, but lack of time would have prevented any real depth in the exchange. It had been one of the greatest frustrations Emily had faced on "Kansas City Morning"—the lack of time and flexibility.

Quinn had taken care of that yesterday by simply ignoring the cues from the control room. He also hadn't left the set during Emily's interviews, and she had been annoyed at first, not only because he seemed to be pushing himself forward, but because he hadn't given her any indication of his intention till it was too late for her to protest.

But her annoyance had quickly passed. He had some good questions, and he didn't trample over hers. In fact, interviewing with Quinn had an easy, natural feeling to it. It was less formal and more chatty, a simple matter of two people getting to know a third.

So, though Emily supposed she could have made a scene and managed to get one-on-one interviews reinstated, she hadn't pressed the point. It was better to save her indignation for something that really mattered.

"Tell me about the movie," Quinn was saying to the guest.

"Tell you? How about me?" Emily put in.

"You've already seen the previews. Remember? You took the tape home last night so I couldn't watch it."

The guest tried in vain to smother his smile. "You couldn't even get your hands on it while Emily was in the shower, Quinn?"

Quinn said earnestly, "I didn't even manage to sneak a peek."

The audience howled with appreciation.

Quinn's eyes widened. "At the *tape,* I meant. Good heavens, what's wrong with you people?"

Emily gave the cue to run the videotape, and by the time the movie clip ended, even the audience seemed to have itself in hand again.

That control didn't last long, of course. The rest of the show was like riding a roller coaster with no brakes, and Emily had never been so happy to hear the closing theme music.

But it wasn't quite over yet. As she waved her special goodbye, Quinn's hand closed around her wrist. "Who are you waving at?" he asked.

"Someone very special."

"I don't doubt it," Quinn murmured, "since you're saying, 'I love you,' in sign language."

The camera caught the sudden flood of color in Emily's cheeks, but mercifully, there wasn't time for anything else. She stepped away from the edge of the set, and the show went black for another day.

"We'd better go out the back way," Quinn said, "or we'll be mobbed." He was still holding her wrist, and he tugged her along with him toward a little-used door at the far side of the studio.

"Are you worried about the audience or Tish?"

He grinned. "A bit of both. Who do you wave at every day?"

"None of your business, Quinn."

"It hadn't dawned on me till just now what you were saying, you know, and suddenly I feel a desperate need for information. If this person you're so attached to is male, six foot six and three hundred pounds, and feels possessive about you..."

Emily stopped outside Jason Manning's office and looked up at Quinn. "Maybe you should have thought of that possibility sooner. See you tomorrow."

She stopped just inside the door of the outer office, her path blocked by two grimy gray mailbags. The bags were empty, but envelopes of every description covered most of the carpet between the desk and the producer's door. In the middle of the mess, kneeling by an enormous heap of mail, was the secretary. She sat back on her heels and brandished her letter opener. "You must want Gary's get-well cards."

Emily nodded. "I had no idea the postal service could be so efficient." And this was just one day's mail. Perhaps she should have accepted Quinn's offer of the RV to haul it over to the hospital.

The secretary thrust a stack of bright-colored envelopes at her. Emily absently leafed through them, straightening the pile. "I'll wait till you've gone through the rest if you like," she offered, "and take them out of your way, too."

The secretary slit a letter-size envelope, glanced at the contents and tossed it onto a heap only slightly smaller than the one she was sorting from. "Most of these aren't for Gary."

"Oh?" Emily felt a painful little twinge in her stomach. If all these letters were complaints, the situation was even worse than she'd anticipated. She'd half expected that yesterday's flurry of telephone calls had been the peak of the protest. "I know some people got excited yesterday, but..."

The secretary picked up half a dozen envelopes. "These are indignant letters, yes." She fanned them like playing cards and tossed them into a chair.

"What about the rest?"

"A mixed bag." The secretary jerked her thumb toward a huge pile to her left. "That stack is requests for tickets to the show. The one over there is fan mail."

"You're kidding."

"And the calls yesterday weren't complaints, either. At least, most of them weren't." She let a handful of envelopes drop into her lap. "The under-thirty crowd, in particular, seems to love the act you and Quinn are putting on."

"Act?" Emily said weakly.

"Whose idea was it for you to behave like a couple of squabbling ten-year-olds, anyway? Not that it matters, Mr. Manning says. Just keep it up."

CHAPTER FOUR

THE TELEPHONE CALLS had been supportive? The letters were actually from fans, not viewers upset by the changes?

Emily read a few of the letters herself and was even more astonished. Such an outpouring of positive response was something she'd never heard of before.

Everyone who worked in television soon learned the mechanics of public reaction. Make an error, let an off-color word slip through, allow a slightly tasteless advertisement to make it onto the air, and the complaints rolled in by the dozens. But if everything went perfectly, the station seldom heard a word of approval. There were often casual compliments, of course; Emily heard them at every public appearance. But those comments were usually general. It was rare to get specific details about what the audience liked, and almost never did someone sit down and write a letter of appreciation. Less often still did they use words like "magical" and "dynamic" and "fascinating."

Emily put the letters back on the pile and tucked Gary's get-well cards into her handbag.

One thing was sure, though. Quinn's plan to get thrown off the show hadn't turned out as he expected. She wondered what he was likely to do next.

In the parking lot, she had to dodge a low-slung bright red sports car headed at high speed for the exit. A few feet past her, the car screeched to a halt, then the driver backed up toward her and lowered his window. "All done for the day?" Brad Jarrett asked.

Did he really think that all she did to earn her pay was smile and chat for two hours every morning? "Hardly."

"I want to talk to you."

Emily glanced at a car that had pulled up behind Brad's, waiting for the lane to be cleared. "You're blocking traffic."

Brad didn't seem to hear the polite beep of the blocked car's horn. His hand tightened on the steering wheel, and his voice was tense. "Is it too much to ask to be treated like a human being on 'Kansas City Morning'?"

Emily was astonished. "I don't know what you mean." From the corner of her eye, she watched the other car back up and take an alternate route to the street.

Brad paid no attention. "Oh, you don't? You chatter with the weather person and give a big buildup to the guests, but when it comes to me it's 'Here's the news' and 'Thanks, Brad,' and on to other things!"

Emily tried to replay the last couple of shows in her mind. "Oh," she said finally. "I guess you're right, though I hadn't noticed."

"I'm being left out, and it isn't fair." He sounded like a sulky child.

"The news is the most serious part of the whole show, Brad. I didn't realize you wanted to be chatty about it. Besides, I'm not the one who's been doing the news introductions."

"I know perfectly well it's Quinn who's been cutting me out. For obvious reasons, of course."

Emily frowned. "Not obvious to me, I'm afraid."

"Why do you think I'm coming in at that ghastly hour of the morning, anyway?"

"Actually, I'd been wondering that."

"It's precisely because news is serious that I can hardly show my whole range of talent on the late news broadcast. But a slot, even a minor one, on 'Kansas City Morning' is a chance to demonstrate what I can really do."

She tried to remember what Brad had said a couple of days ago after Gary's collapse. "I think I see. You intend to— How did you phrase it? Oh, yes. Light fires at the viewers' breakfast tables."

Brad nodded. "Exactly. But Quinn won't let me have a chance."

"Selfish of him, isn't it?" Emily mused.

"If you'd just take things over and give me an opening, I'll do the rest. Then when Jason starts looking for a permanent replacement—" he snapped his fingers "—there I am, already established. We'd be a great combination, honey."

Emily had to bite her tongue because the compliment was so obviously an afterthought. But there was honest curiosity in her voice. "You'd actually give up working in news for 'Kansas City Morning'?"

"What kind of career is this, chasing fire trucks in Kansas City? The best I can hope for if I stay in news is a network foreign-correspondent job, ducking bullets in some godforsaken Third-World country for the rest of my life."

"The networks all have anchors," Emily pointed out dryly. With that boundless ego of his, surely Brad thought he was qualified for the position. She'd be terribly disappointed if he turned modest at this late date.

Brad shook his head. "They're all years away from retiring. I don't have time to wait for that. Besides, I've got my eye on a better deal."

"Like what?"

"Something with national exposure, of course—and not starting at a ghastly hour of the morning, either. A television magazine format, maybe, something that combines my news experience with my interview presence. But in the meantime, 'Kansas City Morning' isn't a bad platform to get some attention while I take a look around.'' He revved the sports car's engine. ''You don't need to tell Jason all that, of course.''

''I wouldn't dream of it.''

''But it wouldn't be fair to let you think I'm planning to stay around forever.''

''How thoughtful of you, Brad. I promise I won't let myself count on you.''

Brad smiled. ''I always like to be up-front where women are concerned. It saves so much trouble in the long run if they don't have unrealistic expectations.''

''Oh, I don't think you need to worry about that with me.''

He gazed at her thoughtfully. Emily had the feeling it might be the first time he'd ever truly seen her. ''Or maybe, if we're as good together as I think we could be, I'll take you up along with me.''

There was no doubt in Emily's mind that he wasn't talking about television. If they were good together, indeed! Of all the slimy propositions...

''Thanks, anyway,'' she said dryly. ''See you around, Brad. You'll be doing the news tomorrow morning, of course?''

''Wouldn't miss the chance for the world.'' The sports car squealed out of the parking lot, leaving the scent of fresh rubber in the air.

Now what? Emily asked herself. Quinn didn't want the job, but he was better at it than she'd ever expected. Brad wanted it desperately, but would he be any good?

The truth was that she didn't care if he was or not. Even if Brad was the best morning-show host ever, working with that ego would be impossible. Still, there wasn't much she could do about the situation.

She stood in the parking lot for several minutes, nibbling on a fingernail, before she remembered that she'd been on her way to the hospital.

"You're losing it, Emily," she muttered. "The stress is taking a toll. You won't have a brain left by the end of the week."

Outside the hospital's intensive-care unit, the same aide she'd talked to on Monday greeted her with an enormous smile. "Good news, Miss Lambert," she said. "We moved Mr. Bennington into a regular room, so he can have visitors any time he feels up to it."

Oh, great, Emily thought. So much for her plans to simply drop off the cards and leave Gary another upbeat note. And if he had seen the show today, she'd have to face questions, and probably anger. "When did he move?"

"As soon as his doctor gave the orders this morning."

"Does he have a television?"

"Oh, yes. All our regular rooms..."

Maybe it wasn't so bad. If Gary had seen the show, he'd have called the station instantly. Since he hadn't called, he must not have seen it. Unless, of course, the switchboard had been gridlocked again and he couldn't get through. That wasn't a comforting thought, and she took a very deep breath before tapping on the door the aide showed her.

Gary was calmly sitting up in bed. His graying hair was neatly combed, his tailored pajamas as neat and fresh as if they'd just been pressed, and he was drinking a cup of broth and paging through a magazine. He might have been lounging in a deck chair in the Caribbean sun, if it wasn't for the intravenous needle in his arm, the monitor over his head that quietly counted off each heartbeat and the sickly bluish cast to his skin.

"I brought your mail," Emily said, waving the bright colored envelopes. "These were delivered to the station."

He eyed the small stack. "That's nice. How's it going?"

"Oh, we're managing." She didn't meet his eyes. "You're looking better." It wasn't quite true, but in circumstances like these, tact was better than brutal honesty.

"The whole thing was an overreaction. I fainted, that's all."

Emily, covertly studying the monitor screen, wasn't quite so certain. The dancing light didn't look like the picture-perfect heart rhythm she'd seen in demonstrations. But she was no professional, and they'd taken him out of intensive care, so he must be better. Besides, Gary himself surely ought to know.

He reached for the cards. "They're opening my mail now?"

"I'm sure Jason wanted to make sure you aren't bothered by business till you're feeling better." She was guiltily aware of the multiple meanings. If one of those fan letters had sneaked into Gary's stack of mail...

He pulled a bright-colored card out and opened it.

"Well, I don't want to tire you out," Emily said. "I'll stop in again tomorrow."

He didn't look up. "With any luck I'll be home in a day or two, and back to work next week."

Which would solve the whole problem. So why didn't she feel happier about it?

Probably because she didn't quite believe his optimism was justified. That blue tint to his skin didn't look right.

The aide, with a nurse beside her, was in the hallway with a cart of supplies. Emily stopped beside them, hesitant to put her intuition into words and yet unable to walk away without inquiring. "Is Mr. Bennington really doing better?"

The aide's hands paused. "Why do you ask?"

Emily shrugged, feeling a little silly. "His color is so bad. And he's still awfully snappish."

The nurse asked, "Isn't he always short-tempered?"

"Not really. Just in the last few weeks." She watched as the nurse thought it over and asked curiously, "Is that important?"

"It might be. People do sometimes get restless and brusque before there's any obvious symptom of a heart attack, and if he's acting strangely again now—"

Emily pounced. "Then he did have a heart attack? He told me he only fainted."

The nurse's eyebrows raised a little. "He didn't just faint, no."

Emily took a deep breath. "If he's really in danger of another attack—"

"I didn't say that," the nurse put in quickly. "He might be curt simply because he's here and not happy about it. Don't worry, he's being watched very closely." She gathered up her supplies and went into a nearby room.

Emily turned to the aide. "Well, just in case, do me a favor, will you? Sabotage his television set."

"Why?"

"Take my word for it. It wouldn't be good for his heart to watch the show."

"But it's such a pleasant little show."

"You obviously haven't watched it for the last couple of days," Emily said grimly.

"No, I've been on the morning shift. But..." The aide sighed. "All right, you've probably got a point. I'll talk to his doctor."

"That's even better." Emily felt some relief as she left the hospital. At least she had done all she could to protect Gary for a while.

She still had to decide what on earth to do about the show.

WHEN EMILY GOT HOME late that afternoon, her grandmother was in the kitchen drinking tea. "Pour yourself a cup," she ordered Emily. "You look as if you're going around in circles."

"You're close, Gran." Emily dropped into a chair and reached for the teapot. "It should have made things easier when Quinn cut the number of guests by half, but it didn't. Now that the interviews are longer, I have to prepare in greater depth, and that takes even more time. I swear I'll never get caught up."

"If you had twice as many hours in the day, you'd manage to fill them up getting ready for tomorrow's show."

"I don't want it to be dull."

"And you don't want to look silly by being unprepared."

Emily smiled. "You're probably right about that. Of course, to top it off, after the show today everything broke loose...."

She'd just started to tell Gran about the sacks full of mail when the front doorbell rang. Carrie pushed her cup away. "Sorry, darling, but that's my fitting."

"Is this the bride who's wearing half a hat? I've got to take a peek at this woman." Emily followed her grandmother down the hall. If her timing was just right, she could get a glimpse of the bride, then whisk herself straight upstairs where she wouldn't be in Gran's way.

Carrie opened the huge old walnut door a few inches, and a soft, sultry feminine voice said, "Oh, I'm late again, aren't I? I hope you'll forgive me, but I brought along someone who's dying to see my wedding dress."

The voice belonged to the kind of woman who could carry off not only that crazy hat but anything else she chose. Still, Emily almost held her breath till Carrie moved back, swinging the door wide.

The woman in the doorway was tall and slender, and she had the huge eyes and high cheekbones of a fashion model. She was gorgeous.

And behind her was not the girlfriend or mother Emily would have expected to be dying to see a wedding dress, but a man. Probably her fiancé, Emily thought, for a woman who could conceive of that hat probably wouldn't be disturbed by the superstition of a man seeing his bride's gown before the ceremony, either.

Then she looked again—at a tall man with dark hazel eyes and sun-streaked brown hair.

"Hello, Quinn," she said.

The woman's eyes widened even more. "Why, it's Emily! I didn't dream ... Quinn was just telling me all about you! What are you doing here? Having a fitting?"

Quinn shook his head at her. "Don't be nosy, Brenna." Then he turned to Emily. "But as long as the question's come up..."

"Emily is my granddaughter," Carrie said. "And this is Brenna Channing, the bride I'm fitting today." She put out a hand to Quinn. "Of course I know who you are, young man."

Brenna Channing laughed, a low and musical ripple of delight. "Because Emily was just telling *her* all about *you,*" she said, and patted Quinn's sleeve in a gesture of mock comfort. "And I can imagine what she was saying, because you were perfectly naughty on the show today." She looked longingly at the pocket doors that separated the hall from the front parlor. "I don't think I can wait another minute. May I, Mrs. Lambert?"

Carrie nodded.

Brenna put a hand on each of the doors and paused for an instant in a dramatic pose. Then she flung the doors wide.

In the center of the room stood a mannequin in a wedding gown fashioned of pale cream silk. The dress was deceptively simple, a sheath with a very narrow skirt, a plain neckline, and a huge bow at the back forming a sort of bustle. Tiny concealed spotlights sparkled off the multitude of beads on the delicate veil, which trailed from the asymmetrical hat.

On most brides, Emily thought, the combination would look like a straitjacket draped with a fishnet. On Brenna Channing, it would be stunning.

Brenna was clinging to Quinn, both hands linked tightly around his arm. "And she did it with nothing more than the photograph," she said almost fiercely. "Can you believe it?"

"Very talented," Quinn said.

Brenna shook him a little. "Oh, don't act that way. Just because it's a wedding gown and you're allergic to the darned things..."

Emily reached for the nearest support. It happened to be a chair, which shifted on the hardwood floor with a sound just short of a squeal. Brenna turned her head and looked at Emily with bright interest in her huge eyes. Then she laughed.

"You thought Quinn's here because he's the groom? Gracious, no. The family considers it a great joke that he's now the Traveling Man, because we've been calling him that for years, where women are concerned."

"Brenna should have been drowned at birth," Quinn said. "Unfortunately the rest of the family didn't see it quite the same way, so they wouldn't let me take care of the problem."

Brenna giggled. "And so I've grown up to be your very favorite cousin."

"Don't push your luck," Quinn recommended. "Are you going to try that thing on or just stand here and drool over it?"

"Don't go away. I'll only be a minute." Brenna stood impatiently beside the mannequin while Carrie unpinned the veil and unbuttoned the back of the gown.

The pocket doors leading to the rear parlor closed behind Brenna and Carrie.

Quinn groaned. "I've heard *that* before. Brenna's sense of time goes out the window whenever she's trying on clothes. She'll probably still be here at midnight."

"Have a seat. Gran's pretty efficient, but I'd say the process will take an hour at least. Still, an hour isn't long if you're dying to see the dress."

"I'm not. Brenna kidnapped me and dragged me over here because she thought your grandmother would make a great feature for the Traveling Man."

"And what do you think?"

"She might be right, if I could work up a proper attitude about wedding gowns. Let's see. The woman who makes every bride's dreams come true..."

Emily considered a tactful silence, but honesty won out. "That's awful, Quinn."

"You're absolutely right." Instead of taking the chair Emily indicated, he leaned against the staircase, his long fingers caressing the smooth carved pineapple that topped the newel post. "What's wrong, Emily?" he said softly.

Her eyes widened in surprise. She hadn't said a word about her concerns; he must have picked it up from her body language. Hadn't she learned to conceal her emotions any better than that? But of course there was no point in trying to hide her feelings from Quinn; this problem concerned him, as well. "Did you see the station's mail today?"

"I heard about it."

"Well, I'd say your scheme backfired." She waited, but he didn't seem inclined to comment. "Actually, to be perfectly accurate, it exploded in your face like a warehouse full of dynamite. You're the hottest thing on morning television."

"Don't you mean *we* are?"

"That's beside the point, don't you think? *I* like the job. What are you going to do, Quinn?"

"I think . . ." He frowned. "I can reason more clearly after I've had some ice cream. Didn't I see a little shop up the street?"

"Is that why you did a story on the factory a couple of weeks ago? Just so you could get free samples?"

Quinn shrugged. "It's a tough job, but somebody's got to take it on. Come with me. Brenna will never miss us."

Spring was in the air; the breeze was soft and almost warm, and next to the sidewalks tiny flower shoots were standing like soldiers at attention, not quite ready to unfurl their leaves and petals.

"Are you certain you don't want to go on location?" Quinn asked.

Emily glared at him.

The ice-cream shop was quiet. Quinn ordered a double dip of a concoction called Chocoholic's Delight, and frowned at Emily's request. "Can't you find anything more original in that whole array of flavors than lemon sherbet in a paper cup?" He appealed to the young man behind the counter. "What's the most unusual flavor you have?"

The young man didn't even stop to think. "That would have to be the jalapeño pepper."

Quinn looked a little doubtful. "Do you sell a lot of it?"

"No."

"Now that's a story for you," Emily murmured. "I can't wait to see you trying it on camera."

"Oh, eat your lemon sherbet." Quinn settled into a booth and bit into his ice cream with evident enjoyment.

Emily dug her spoon into the side of her sherbet. "Quinn," she said slowly, "would you please stop trying to get off the show, and . . . and just stay?"

He looked at her over the top of his cone. The mischievous light dawned in his eyes and he started to smile. "Why, Emily, I didn't know you cared!"

"It's not out of any great fondness for you," Emily snapped. "But the alternative is a whole lot worse." She took a deep breath and told him about Brad's ambitions.

Quinn didn't answer; he only released a long, slow tuneless whistle and finished off his ice cream, crunching each bite of his cone as if he enjoyed the destruction, until Emily couldn't stand it any longer.

"Well?" she said. "What am I supposed to do about Brad?"

Quinn's eyebrows lifted a fraction. "Do? Just as he asked, of course. Starting tomorrow, you'll introduce the news."

And that, to Emily's frustration, was all he would say.

IT DIDN'T OCCUR to Emily until the next morning that Quinn might have meant he wasn't going to turn up at all, so she'd have to introduce not only the news but everything else, as well. But when she came into the studio a few minutes before air time, Quinn was already there, signing autographs for the audience. Emily tried to smother her sigh of relief.

Her suspicions had been silly, anyway. No matter how much Quinn disliked "Kansas City Morning," going on strike wasn't a good way to protest. The Traveling Man was likely to end up without a job at all.

There was hardly an empty seat to be found in Studio B, and the crowd buzzed with excitement. The enthusiasm was contagious, and when Quinn joined her on the tall chairs for the first segment of the show, Emily gave him a brilliant smile.

He blinked a little, and as soon as the opening credits had rolled, he said, "Well, if there's any power shortage on the set today, Tish can just start plugging the lights into you. What's the reason for this glow you've got, Emily dear?"

Good question, she thought. Why was she suddenly so certain things would work out? Simply because Quinn hadn't deserted her? "Well, it's a beautiful morning. And our audience today is full of energy. Can't you feel it?"

Quinn nodded. "Of course I can. And yesterday was a red-letter day, too."

"What?"

His gaze was full of disappointment. "Surely you haven't forgotten?" He leaned forward and confided to the audience, "Emily introduced me to her grandmother."

The reaction was instantaneous, like a delicious shiver running through the entire crowd. It wasn't surprising, though; he'd made it sound as if she'd invited him over for family approval!

Quinn settled back into his chair. "You've got a very talented grandmother."

If he says a word about wedding gowns, she thought, I'll strangle him with the nearest cable. "Gran is special," she admitted cautiously.

"Very. She's the one you wave to at the end of every show, isn't she?"

"Now why would you think that?"

Quinn gently tweaked her earlobe. "Because she's the neatest grandmother I've ever met. In fact, if she was mine, I'd wave at her, too."

"I still don't see why you should jump to the conclusion that I'm waving at her and not someone else."

"Like a man?" Quinn's tone said he scoffed at the idea.

Emily bristled. "Wait a minute. Don't assume there isn't a man in my life, Quinn."

He leaned a little closer. "Of course there's a man in your life, darling. Me."

A collective sigh swept through the studio audience.

"Now, listen," Emily ordered, "I don't want to make waves here, but—"

"You could create a tidal wave in a dishpan, Emily, so when it comes to vulnerable males like me—"

She ignored him and looked out over the crowd. "There is absolutely nothing between Quinn and me."

The audience shrieked with laughter.

The corner of Quinn's mouth quirked. He tapped his index fingertip against his jaw and waited patiently for the hilarity to die down. Then he said earnestly, "My mother always told me never to contradict a lady in public, so I think we'd better change the subject, don't you?" He propped his elbow on the back of her chair and said confidentially, "Don't forget the news, Emily. Poor Brad's been waiting for ages."

After that sort of lead-in, anything Brad Jarrett said, no matter how brilliant, would have sounded somewhat flat. But he tried hard, Emily had to admit. He complimented her dress, and he teased her—rather heavily, she thought, but then, perhaps she was prejudiced; the audience seemed to enjoy it. And after the news, instead of handing things back to the studio as he was supposed to, he introduced the weather report himself and started bantering with Robin.

Tish Grant was in the control room making frantic faces, which of course Brad couldn't see. Even if he could, Emily suspected, he wouldn't have paid any attention. The director looked as if she were about to explode. If things went on along this path, Emily thought, Tish was apt to end up in the hospital room next to Gary's.

But finally Brad ran down. The technician in the weather room, taken aback by the departure from normal, had apparently been fiddling with the camera angles, and suddenly Robin was on the air again, calm and professional as always—but for the first time very obviously pregnant.

Emily sighed and fervently hoped that the hospital aide had kept her word and managed to remove Gary's television set. He had insisted on the tight camera angles, arguing that Robin's increasing girth would only distract the audience.

Quinn seemed to read her mind. "The baby wasn't going to stay invisible forever," he said.

"I know. And we can hardly ignore it now, can we?"

He looked directly at the camera as Robin finished giving the extended forecast. "That was quite an announcement, Robin, and you didn't even say a word. When's the baby due?"

"Another month." Robin didn't sound surprised by the question; she must have caught a glimpse of herself on the monitor.

"Is it a boy or a girl?"

"I don't know, and I don't care, because I just want a healthy baby. We haven't even chosen names, so . . ."

Quinn's eyes widened dramatically, and he turned to Emily. "Then we'll have to help out. Maybe we should have a contest, and the best name submitted for Robin Wright's

ew baby will win." He frowned. "What should the grand
prize be, do you think?"

Emily was holding her breath. He might come up with
anything, from a free Lamaze class to a trip to Disneyland,
and then Tish would really have apoplexy.

"We'll work the rules out and let you know," Quinn
promised, and Emily started breathing again. Before things
could deteriorate any further, she moved on to the first
guest.

"In a city this size, there are always good causes in need
of money," she began. "And combining fun with fund-
raising is always a challenge." She turned to Quinn. "Have
you noticed that when there's a charity function that really
sounds entertaining, it's often Whitney Townsend's name
at the head of the organizers? Whitney's here with us today
to talk about a celebrity auction on Saturday night." She
rose and moved across the stage to greet a dark-haired young
woman in a simple business suit.

There was always a little bustle involved in greeting a
guest, exchanging kisses and handshakes and getting the
person settled. Emily was grateful for the tall chairs; usually by this time her back would be starting to ache from
sitting on the love seat.

"What do you sell at a celebrity auction?" she asked.
"Surely not celebrities!"

The dark-haired young woman laughed. "Not precisely.
We're auctioning lunch with the mayor, for instance, and a
baseball signed by the entire Kansas City Royals pitching
staff, and the manuscript of a book by a well-known local
author. There will be something for everyone, from historical autographs to tickets and backstage passes for the
Hunter Dix concert next month."

"And the money you raise?"

"We support programs to help teach job skills to disad
vantaged youth. It's a wonderful cause, and it's also going
to be a fun occasion. We're counting on Quinn for that—
he's the emcee, official host and auctioneer."

Emily put a hand on Quinn's arm. "You didn't tell me
you were involved in this!"

Quinn gave her a look of outraged innocence. "You just
told the world that there's nothing between us, so I didn'
think there'd be a problem if I made plans for Saturday
night."

"That wasn't what I meant. I'm just stunned that you're
going to try to be an auctioneer."

"Try? I'll have you know I'm almost a pro. Remember
last year when I did the piece on the auctioneer's school?"

"No."

"Too bad. It was a great story. I learned the basics then.
They actually teach people how to carry on that constant
singsong patter and breathe at the same time."

"I can't believe you needed to be taught *that*. How about
giving us a demonstration?"

"Oh, no. If you want to see me work, you can buy a ticket
for Saturday night."

Whitney said, "We'd be delighted to have you cohost,
Emily."

Quinn frowned. "I was selling tickets for you, Whitney.
You won't make any money giving them away."

Whitney ignored him. "Men who buy items would much
rather get a kiss of congratulations from you, Emily, than
from Quinn."

Quinn rubbed a knuckle across his jaw. "This is what
happens when you let women gang up on you."

"Maybe I'll donate something," Emily mused. "Do you
have any suggestions?"

"A tour of the studio and station," Whitney suggested. "Or a dress you've worn on the show..."

"A date," Quinn put in. "Except it would be awfully inconvenient for you to go out to dinner when you're always in bed by ten."

The audience gave a gentle sigh.

"Ah," Quinn murmured. "You're wondering how I know." He smiled angelically and let the silence drag out.

In self-defense, Emily said, "I told him."

There was a spattering of laughter, and some applause.

"I'm serious," she protested.

The laughter grew stronger. Even their guest was obviously having trouble keeping a straight face.

Emily gave up. This was getting out of hand!

CHAPTER FIVE

WHAT A WEEK, Emily thought at the end of the show, as they walked to the edge of the set and waved goodbye to the cameras and the studio audience. Just last Friday her life had been normal, and now...

She noticed that Quinn, too, was waving the sign-language code for "I love you."

"Who's that for?" she asked over the applause. "The woman in your life?"

Quinn nodded. "All of them," he confided. "I'm trying to make you jealous."

The camera's signal light went off. "Are you ever going to let me have the last word, Quinn?" Emily paused outside the studio's back door. "Seriously, I need to talk—"

Jason Manning came down the hall, his face aglow. "Great idea of yours, you two—teaming up on the celebrity-auction thing."

"If you think it over, Jason," Emily said, "you'll realize it wasn't either of us but Whitney Townsend who came up with that brainstorm."

Jason waved a dismissing hand. "Well, whoever did, it's a magnificent opportunity."

"No wonder her fund-raisers are so successful," Emily muttered. "The woman's a hypnotist."

Quinn grinned at her. "The auction starts at nine in the evening. I'll pick you up." He started for the door.

"Quinn, I really need to talk to you!"

He glanced at his watch. "Honey, the crew's already waiting for me."

"Crew?"

"Remember? Unlike you, I still have my other job."

"Oh." Emily bit her lip. "I forgot."

"You *forgot?*" He came toward her, his tweed jacket pushed back and his hands on his hips. "Fifteen minutes ago, when the Traveling Man segment aired, you told me it was wonderful."

"It was. I assumed you had a backlog of stories on tape."

"I do, but they're going to be used up very soon at this rate, so I'm going out to shoot some more. What do you need to talk about? I can squeeze in five minutes."

"I want to discuss the show. And five minutes isn't going to be long enough. Will you call me when you get back?"

"I can't promise when it will be. We're going to have a long day trying to catch up with a week's work."

Emily sighed. "Tomorrow, then. Before the auction."

"That's going to be crazy, too." He was loosening his tie as he spoke. "Why not grab your stuff and come along?"

"On your shoot?" Her voice was incredulous. "I can't."

"What's keeping you here? You don't have any public appearances. I checked before I scheduled this trip, in case you needed me."

"In case I *needed* you? Honestly, Quinn . . ."

He grinned. "If all you're doing today is getting ready for next week's shows, there's no reason you can't read while we're taping."

That was true enough, she supposed. And it was important that she talk to him before the celebrity auction. This situation was already outlandish enough, but it was still possible to get things back in hand. At the auction, however, in front of a live audience and without the restraints of television, Quinn might say or do anything, and then the damage to "Kansas City Morning" might be irreversible.

"It will be nice and quiet," Quinn said, "and we can talk on the road."

"All right. Let me get out of this dress . . ." She started to color as she heard what she'd said.

But Quinn, for a change, didn't jump on the double meaning. "Just pick up your clothes. You can change once we get rolling."

"Oh, we're taking the infamous recreational vehicle?" She didn't wait for an answer, just headed for her dressing room and tossed everything she might conceivably need into her backpack.

The RV was waiting in the parking lot, engine running. Though it wasn't the largest one Emily had ever seen, it was a far cry from the economy model. It also sat farther above the ground than she'd bargained for, and her high-heeled pumps and narrow skirt presented a challenge when she tried to reach the step. "I knew you should have waited for me to change," she muttered.

"We didn't have an hour to kill." Quinn tossed her backpack into the vehicle, then caught her around the waist and set her up into the doorway with no apparent effort.

Emily made a grab for the hem of her skirt, which had slid upward with terrifying speed as he lifted her. "I don't ever take an hour to get dressed."

"Well, my only experience with you is in the mornings, that's true." He stepped up beside her, so close in the narrow doorway that she was practically pressed against him. "Wave nicely to the onlookers, Emily."

Emily had forgotten that the studio audience was still trickling out of the station. She groaned. "This isn't such a hot idea, you know. We're leaving the world with the impression that we're joined at the wrist!"

Quinn shrugged. "If it amuses them, what's the harm?" He pointed at the two men in the front seats of the RV. "Ivan, the technician, and Murray, the cameraman—this is Emily, who's along for the ride." He opened a narrow closet door, pulled his tie off and draped it over a hook. "Let's get rolling."

As the RV lurched out of the parking lot, he ushered Emily back to the kitchen, midway down the length of the vehicle. "Bath's through there." He pointed to a door.

Emily opened it. "Oh, joy," she said. "It gives new meaning to the word 'cramped.' This makes airplane rest rooms look like the Ritz."

"So change out here."

"I know, you promise to close your eyes. Well, thanks, Quinn, but—"

"Nope," Quinn said. "I didn't promise anything of the sort." He pulled open a cabinet door. "You see, I'm in charge of the galley, and the crew will mutiny if their doughnuts don't arrive on schedule."

By the time Emily maneuvered herself into her jeans and returned to the kitchen, a cup of coffee was waiting for her in a deep indentation cut in the small table. She settled down on the upholstered bench. "It's a good thing I've done a bit of yoga along the way, or I'd be stuck in there yet."

She looked around the vehicle. From the outside, she'd have expected more room, somehow, but the interior was compact and full of fitted cabinets and compartments. Toward the back of the vehicle, she spotted the corner of a bed; it occupied almost every inch of the rear cubicle and was separated from the kitchen by a curtain. That wouldn't have been much better as a changing room, she decided; she'd have had to stand on the bed itself. Or more likely kneel, because the ceilings were so low that Quinn had to be careful as he moved around.

She sipped her coffee. "When you're out for days, where do you all sleep?"

"The table folds up and the benches slide out to make a berth, and another one drops down from the wall."

"Bunk beds. Every little boy's dream."

"But not terribly comfortable for anyone over four feet tall and fifty pounds, I'm afraid."

"Where are we going, anyway?"

"West—out the Kansas Turnpike to the Topeka area. I've got four stories lined up out there."

"Four?"

"It's more efficient that way. I did warn you we might be late, didn't I?"

"Yes, but I didn't think. I should have called—" She stopped.

"Your grandmother, I suppose? There's a cellular phone in that cupboard."

There was no sense in being irritated because he'd jumped to the conclusion that she was checking in with Gran, not canceling a date; he was right, after all. "You don't usually shoot in bunches like this, do you?"

"Sometimes. We just don't show the stories in sequence, so it looks as if we've been wandering the Midwest like Gypsies. But right now we don't have the leisure to trail across four states looking for variety, so we take what we can get."

"That makes it tougher, I'm sure."

"Oh, yes. I had my schedule all lined up, too. I was supposed to be in Iowa this week doing a story on Albert, the world's largest bull."

Emily tried to keep a straight face. "How disappointed you must be to miss that."

Quinn nodded. "Yes, but he'll still be there when I get around to him. He's made of concrete." He added hot coffee to his cup and settled down across the table from her. "What's up, Emily? Or was the talk an excuse, and you hitched this ride for the joy of my company?"

"Don't flatter yourself." She looked down at her coffee. He'd filled the cup only halfway; a good thing, too, as the RV's motion had already set the liquid swaying. "I'm worried about Gary."

"I thought Jason said he was doing better."

"He is, but..." She told him about her visit to the hospital yesterday, and Gary's odd bluish color, and the monitors, and what the aide had said about his snappishness. "The thing that really worries me is the show," she finished. "If he isn't over the worst, and he sees what we've done to his show..."

"You actually think the shock would kill him? Oh, come on, Emily. He didn't have any complaints this morning, or Jason would have heard about it."

Emily admitted, "I arranged it so Gary didn't have a television."

"My, you are Little Miss Fixit, aren't you?"

"Well, somebody's got to take care of these things. Jason doesn't even seem to be worried."

Quinn cradled his coffee mug in one long brown hand. "Maybe he knows something you don't."

"Like what? You mean, he might think it doesn't matter because he's sure Gary's not coming back?"

"Maybe."

She shook her head. "Before he collapsed, Gary had no intention of leaving the show any time soon. I'd swear to that. And afterward, well, maybe he said something of the sort, but people say lots of things they don't mean when they've had that kind of shock. Jason wouldn't take it seriously. And if he knows Gary won't be physically fit to come back, he'd have told me, wouldn't he? He might not make a public announcement yet, but why keep it a secret from me?''

Quinn shrugged. "It's just an idea. I might be way off base. Anyway, why are you kicking up such a fuss about the show? You're the one who wanted to make changes.''

Emily was stunned. "*I* wanted? What do you mean?''

"You were telling me all about it in the commissary the other day," he reminded her. "Before Gary went down for the count.''

"I wasn't giving details. And the changes I was talking about would be under very different circumstances. If Gary retired, I'd stir things up so fast—''

"That's what I thought. And you can't say you haven't been helping to stir them up now.''

"Not intentionally. Things have been moving so quickly all week it's been like riding a tornado, Quinn, and you know it. And the cases aren't the same, anyway. Once Gary's retired, I'd be changing my own show, not his, so it wouldn't be disrespectful to him. But under these circumstances, when he's sick, it's an insult to make his show into something else.''

"So what do you suggest?''

"Well, if we toned down the nonsense and simply did the job... No more outrageous flirting and mad exaggerations...''

He looked thoughtful. "You mean, you don't want me to close Monday's show with a comment about the gorgeous wedding gown your grandmother's making?''

She could hear the tone he'd use, too, soft and sultry and suggestive, and the listeners would swear he was talking about a very personal wedding. "That is precisely the sort of thing I'm talking about," she said firmly. "It creates havoc and doesn't do a thing for anybody.''

"It seems to entertain a few people.''

"Oh, the audience is intrigued by the banter, and who wouldn't be? But—"

"Exactly. So what are you complaining about?"

"It's not our show to tinker with, Quinn. It's Gary's. He built it, and it's not fair of us to shake the foundations the minute his back is turned—and while he's sick, at that." Quinn was frowning; Emily took a deep breath and pressed her advantage. "You wouldn't like it if someone took your place as the Traveling Man for a couple of weeks and turned it into a gossip piece with a new scandal every day."

"Nobody could take my place," he said mildly.

"And until Gary has said—if he does—that he isn't coming back, it's not only rude, it's cruel to do what we've done. It's like giving someone's whole wardrobe to the Salvation Army before he's quite dead."

Quinn said slowly, "I hadn't looked at it that way, exactly." He took a long drink of coffee. "Still, I think you're wrong. It's not Gary's show anymore—" He held up a hand as she started to protest. "Hear me out, Emily. In any kind of group, when there's a change in the people involved, things are different afterward. Not better, necessarily, or worse—just different."

Emily couldn't deny that. "I suppose so."

"For instance, if Tish quit and someone else took over as director, there'd soon be a new flavor on the show, right?"

"I don't quite see your point."

"What's so bad about us being ourselves? We can't pretend to be Gary's clones, you know. If we try, we'll be the biggest flops in town, and I'm not wild about looking like a fool. So why not do what we're best at?"

Emily bit her lip. She hated to admit that his argument made sense. But it still didn't feel right.

"When Gary comes back, it'll be different again. He'll keep what he likes and maybe have a few new ideas of his own. It's not as if we've done anything irreversible. What's the worst that can happen, anyway? Gary throws out our chairs?''

"He'll hate the studio audience."

"Maybe. But if you're suggesting we cancel it now, forget it—the tickets are already spoken for. Besides, we're dynamite with an audience, and you know it."

Emily nodded reluctantly. "I suppose you're right about that. But—"

"Then it's settled. Now if we're not going to have a starving crew on our hands, I'd better organize lunch." He drained his mug.

She gave up. "Can I help?"

"Not really. The kitchen's too small, and unless you've got your road legs..."

"It's sort of like walking on a boat deck, isn't it?"

"Exactly." He moved efficiently around the kitchenette, slicing bread, then adding thick stacks of deli cold cuts, tomato slices, cheese and lettuce, and wrapping each sandwich in waxed paper.

Emily watched in mild surprise. She'd run into a few big names since she moved into television, and she couldn't think of a single one who would consider waiting on his crew like this. After all, Quinn was the star of the show; most people in his position would expect the crew to take care of him. And even lesser-known personalities seemed to assume that because they were actually on the air, they were more important than the people behind the scenes; it was almost funny to think of Brad Jarrett fixing lunch for his camera crew. But Quinn was obviously at home in the tiny kitchen.

"You seem to have a good organization," she said finally.

"Oh, this is a great team. With Murray and Ivan, I can get more done in two days than any other crew could accomplish in a week."

"Do you do kitchen duty often?"

"Most of the time. Murray and Ivan share the driving, so I can stay fresh and rested and looking lovely for the camera. Providing breakfast, lunch and snacks is my part of the job." He stacked the sandwiches on a tray and got mugs down from a high cabinet. "When we've got a list of stories to do, we can cover a lot more territory if we don't have to search for restaurants. On the other hand, when we have time to wander around and look for ideas, we'll stop at every coffee shop we can find and shoot the breeze with the locals."

"Not a bad life-style."

"It has its moments. A couple of weeks ago we parked overnight at a lake and Murray pulled in a bunch of trout for dinner. But most of the time it's not quite so lush."

She watched as he opened a vacuum bottle, and caught a rich beefy scent as he parceled out soup into the mugs.

"What did you do before?" she asked. "You can't always have been the Traveling Man."

He looked over his shoulder at her with one eyebrow raised.

Emily felt a bit stupid. "Well, maybe I should know," she said defensively, "but I don't. I really didn't watch the station much before I started working there, so—"

"News," Quinn said briefly. "But it wasn't in Kansas City. Want some soup?"

"Please. How long have you been here?"

"This time around? Four years or so."

Her soup was still steaming, so she blew gently on the surface. "Then you grew up here? Since your cousin's here, too, I assumed . . ."

He nodded. "Excuse me for a minute." He picked up the tray of sandwiches and soup and disappeared toward the front of the vehicle. When he came back, he put a sandwich in front of Emily and moved her backpack so he could sit down across from her. "What have you got in that bag, anyway? It weighs a ton."

"Mostly books."

"Are we interviewing that many authors next week?"

"No, but I have to read a lot to keep up with all of the other subjects, too. Now that we're both sitting in on interviews and doing them in more depth, it's turned into twice the work." She nibbled at her sandwich. "How do you manage, with all this to do, too?"

Quinn shrugged. "I may resort to reading only the right-hand pages. By the way, if you want to use the videotape machine..."

"I saw you've got one." It occupied a shelf in the partition between the kitchen and the rear bedroom compartment.

"It takes power from the RV's batteries, so it's better to leave the engine running if you want to watch a tape."

"Isn't that a nuisance if you guys want to have a film fest?"

He grinned. "I told you the life-style isn't always grand."

The hum of the engine and of the tires against the pavement shifted suddenly as the RV left the highway, and the angle of the turn made Emily grab the table for balance. "Do you ever get used to the noise and the motion?" she asked.

"Oh, yes. Eventually." He looked out the window. "Darn it, I miscalculated. I thought we'd be another fifteen minutes getting here." He pushed the rest of his sandwich aside, opened a compartment door and pulled out a fresh shirt and a pullover. "We're going to be here a couple of hours at least."

"I've got plenty to do." But Emily didn't reach for her backpack. She finished the last few bites of her sandwich, then sipped the dregs of her coffee and watched as Quinn unbuttoned his shirt and put on the fresh one. His chest was broad and surprisingly tanned, considering the season, and she wondered idly if the dark hair that covered his skin was as soft as it looked. She didn't realize she was watching him till he pulled the sweater over his head and shook a warning finger at her.

"You didn't close your eyes," he said, and then he was gone. A couple of minutes later, the RV's door slammed, and silence descended.

Emily peeked out the window as the cameraman and technician began assembling equipment. They had pulled into the driveway of a small, square white house in a middle-class neighborhood; there was nothing obvious that set the house apart from its neighbors. She watched as Quinn knocked on the door and was welcomed by a tiny woman whose wrinkled face made her look a thousand years old, and they vanished inside.

Emily rewrapped his sandwich so it wouldn't dry out and put it in the tiny refrigerator, then emptied her backpack onto the table and surveyed the preparations for the next week. First things first, of course; Monday's show would include a retired politician who had written his memoirs.

By the time the shoot was finished, Emily had stretched her legs the length of the little bench and propped her spine against the window. If it hadn't been for the sheer discomfort of the position, she'd have had to fight to keep her eyes open; the politician ought to have hired a ghostwriter. But the noise of the equipment being reloaded brought her fully awake.

"How's it going?" Quinn asked as the RV lurched onto the road again. He poured himself another cup of coffee, then investigated the refrigerator and found the remains of his lunch.

Emily shut the book with a snap. "I'm about to try your suggestion and skip every other page."

"I find it adds a certain amount of challenge and keeps the mind focused." Quinn looked at the title on the dust jacket. "I'm glad you're reading this one so I don't have to."

"You're the one who wanted to team up on interviews, Quinn. How did the story go?"

"It'll be good. That sweet old woman has been painting and decorating eggs for years, and the house is lined with them. Chicken eggs, goose eggs, even ostrich eggs. She's Topeka's version of Fabergé."

"Perfect timing with Easter coming up next week. How do you find all these unusual people, Quinn? I know, I know—you ask the locals in the coffee shops."

"Sometimes. Or they write the station, or their friends do."

A car passed the RV, its teenage passengers leaning out the windows, shrieking and waving.

"You can't exactly sneak around town in this thing, can you?" Emily said wryly. "With the station logo on the side and all the antennas and pictures of the whole rig on the air twice a day..."

"It's like trying to hide an aircraft carrier in a swimming pool." Quinn waved at the kids.

"The only thing lacking is a bullhorn blaring, 'Make way for the Traveling Man!'"

"Don't tell the station manager or he'll order one."

Emily shifted on the bench. "For all the size of this thing, it's not very comfortable in here."

"Oh, if you really want a challenge, try being six inches taller."

"No, thanks." She studied him thoughtfully. He looked tired, as if he had poured tremendous energy into shooting the Easter-egg story. "At least that's one of the four out of the way."

"Well, sort of. Two hours of shooting leaves me with about an hour of tape."

"And that has to be edited down to what? Five minutes?"

"Nothing to it," Quinn said dryly.

"You do the editing yourself, too?"

"Of course. That's what makes a good story stand out from an ordinary one, Emily. Anybody can ask questions and take pictures, but it's the cutting and pasting that make it special."

"When will you do that?"

Quinn sighed. "Tomorrow. Four stories, two versions of each. If I'm lucky I'll be done by the time the auction starts. Otherwise, Sunday's shot, too."

Even Emily, who ought to have known better, had never stopped to think about the work involved behind the scenes in making those tiny light features of his. That, she realized, was because the craftsmanship was so perfect that the effort never showed on the air. Each of Quinn's stories had a graceful ease, a seamlessness, as if it had just fallen into place with no one troubling over it at all. That was part of the magic of the Traveling Man, of course—and part of Quinn's skill.

"I can understand why getting up at four to do 'Kansas City Morning' isn't at the top of your list," she said.

Quinn yawned. "Now see what you've done? You reminded me."

"I'm sorry I've been a little hard on you about the difficulties of live TV. Compared to this..."

"Sometimes, I have to admit, having only one shot at it is a relief. Right or wrong, at least it's done." He got up to rummage in a drawer and pulled out a package of cookies. "But I seem to have a knack for this kind of thing, so..."

Emily shook her head at the cookies. Quinn took a handful and passed the rest of the package up to the driver.

She doodled a rectangle on her notepad. "It's a whole lot more than a knack," she said. "It's an incredible gift for feel-good stories."

"Please, Emily. Can't you see I'm blushing?"

She wasn't listening. "That's not all, either. You never do a piece that makes fun of anyone. If that Easter-egg collection was the tackiest thing west of the Mississippi, you'd still make the owner look like a craftsman."

"It's a good thing we're not going far. I'd be a whimpering puddle on the floor if you kept this up for another ten minutes." He dug a sport coat and tie out of the closet. "I hope you'll be feeling more like yourself by the time I come back, Emily."

The RV had scarcely stopped before he was swinging down from the door.

"He's acting as if I've stumbled across his guilty secret," Emily murmured. And in a sense she had. It would be so easy with many of Quinn's stories to add a tongue-in-cheek twist, a sort of private joke between him and the viewer, with the butt being the subject of the story. It would be easy—and sometimes the prospect must be inviting. Most reporters wouldn't hesitate to make themselves look smarter, or higher class, or better educated, by laughing ever so slightly at the foibles of the people they interviewed.

But Quinn wasn't like that at all. He was genuinely fascinated by the nutty things people did. And since he didn't feel he was better than the people he interviewed, he wasn't even tempted to score points at their expense. The result was heartwarming; after she saw that piece on the Topeka woman, Emily might not want to start decorating eggs herself, but she would respect the devotion and care the woman poured into her hobby.

No wonder Quinn was so good at what he did. And no wonder he didn't want to mess it up for the sake of "Kansas City Morning." But of course this double duty wouldn't last long. Gary would soon be well and back in his place, and Quinn would be free to roam once more.

So why didn't she feel wholeheartedly happy about it?

CHAPTER SIX

EMILY COULD NOT concentrate on the politician's memoirs. Eventually she pushed aside the book and dug a manicure kit out of her backpack. If she was going to be glamorous at the celebrity auction tomorrow, freshly done nails wouldn't be a bad place to start.

Besides, perhaps it wasn't necessary to do all the research she'd habitually waded through for each guest. She couldn't stop reading their work altogether, of course; she could hardly ask intelligent questions if she had no information to base them on. But since the viewers hadn't read every book or studied every topic, maybe it would be better to stick to basics. She might be able to learn something from Quinn; if she could acquire that knack of his for asking artless questions...

"That's probably not as easy as it looks, either," she muttered. And of course the Traveling Man had the distinct advantage of videotape; if his question came out sounding dumb, he could edit it out and use only the answer.

She was just putting on the final coat of polish when Quinn came back to the RV.

"Whew!" he said. "What are you doing in here? Refinishing furniture?"

"Sorry." Emily waved a hand to clear the air, tipped over the bottle of nail polish and scrambled to set it upright before the liquid could pour over the table. "I didn't realize the smell would be so overpowering in such a small space."

He cranked open a couple of windows. "Why do you women go through such antics to be attractive, anyway?"

Emily glared at him. "To preserve the illusions of men, of course." She had caught a nail on the corner of the table in her effort to prevent a spill, and its glossy surface was marred beyond repair. "Maybe if men understood what an effort it is, they'd be more understanding when women fall short of the impossible ideal."

"Sounds like a good topic for the show." He pulled his tie loose, rolled up his sleeves and turned the water on in the tiny kitchen sink. "Of course, men do lots of things for women, too." He put his head under the faucet.

Emily watched in sheer envy. If she stuck her head in the sink between appearances, she'd be twenty minutes just getting her makeup straightened out. Anyone who had the gall to pull that stunt had no business talking about the ways men went out of their way to be attractive to women!

"Name one," she demanded.

Quinn came up for air and groped for a towel. "That's easy, Emily. Neckties. You don't think it was a man who invented these things, do you?"

"I've never considered it important enough to wonder about."

"Of course you haven't, because you don't have to wear one."

She studied her ruined nail. She couldn't even wipe the polish off and start over; Quinn would have a fit if she opened another bottle. "You know," she mused, "with Father's Day coming up in a couple of months..."

Quinn stopped rubbing his hair. It stood up in damp peaks. "What now?"

"We could have an 'awful necktie' contest. Wouldn't that be funny? Have men send in the worst neckties they ever owned. We can select the finalists, and the Friday before Father's Day the studio audience can choose the big winner."

"And pictures," Quinn said. "Each contestant wearing his entry."

Emily nodded eagerly. "And a letter about how he happened to get this particular tie. This is great, Quinn!"

"Well, run it past Gary and see what he says."

Emily's enthusiasm vanished like the air from a popped balloon. Father's Day was still eight or nine weeks away, and for a moment, she had forgotten that Gary would almost certainly be back by then. She could almost hear what he'd say about her idea. And as for the studio audience being the judges . . .

Not likely, she thought, and tried to cheer herself with the thought that someday she'd be free to have as many lighthearted contests as she wanted.

They stopped at a small restaurant in Topeka for an early dinner. "We'll be asphyxiated if we spend any more time in the RV," Quinn said. "Let's give it a while to air out."

Emily would have argued, just on the principle of the thing—he didn't need to imply that she'd messed up the air in his precious RV on purpose!—except that she was hungry. Besides, the fumes had given her a headache and she'd rather not admit it.

Inside the restaurant, half a dozen people asked for Quinn's autograph. Ivan and Murray ignored the interruptions and finished their salads; obviously they were used to Quinn's getting attention. Emily rolled her eyes a little.

Quinn signed a paper napkin and handed it back to the teenage boy who had brought it to the table. "Don't feel bad that they don't recognize you, darling," he murmured. "I'm doing my best to bring you to public notice."

"I don't feel bad about it at all," Emily said crisply. "I'm positive they only know it's you because of that massive house-on-wheels parked outside."

Quinn frowned. "And all this time I've thought it was my handsome face the public loved."

She relented a little. "Well, perhaps they know your face, once the RV has reminded them of you. You're on the air at enough oddly assorted times to build up a following. Did you know that some people assume you're actually at the station every time one of your stories runs? When do they think you sleep, I wonder?"

Quinn yawned. "I'd like the answer to that question myself. One more story and we can head for home."

"But you've only done two, haven't you?"

"We shot the last one as a two-part series. That's why it took so long—or did the nail polish do such a number on your brain you didn't notice?"

They lingered over coffee and dessert, and Emily, who was enjoying Ivan's dry humor and Murray's stock of stories, was sorry when Quinn reached for the bill and his wallet.

Their waitress fluttered over to the table and picked up his credit card. "If you wouldn't mind awfully, Mr. Randolph," she said hesitantly, "could I have a dollar bill as part of my tip, and would you sign it? I collect autographed bills, you see."

"How about checks?" Ivan asked.

Quinn silenced him with a look and obliged, signing his name with a flourish. "That's flattering, you know," he said as they climbed into the RV once more. "She was willing to give up part of what she earns to get my autograph. In a way, it's as if she paid for it."

Emily said sweetly, "At least she knows your autograph will always be worth something. The boy with the napkin, on the other hand..."

"You're just jealous because no one paid any attention to you in your jeans and ponytail," Quinn said.

"And that proves my argument that women have a tougher time living up to men's expectations than men do living up to women's. Neckties, indeed!"

The argument went on till they reached their next destination. Emily enjoyed it, and the sudden silence that descended on the RV after Quinn and the crew had unpacked once more dampened her spirits.

She settled down at the table with her book again. But it was dark outside now, and the lights in the kitchenette were completely inadequate. Just trying to find her way through the politician's memoirs had been difficult enough without adding eyestrain.

She glanced into the rear compartment and saw a high-intensity spotlight in one corner, perfectly positioned for reading in bed. She took one more look out the window, noting that Quinn and the crew were already out of sight. So she piled up the pillows and snuggled down on the bed. "Why didn't I think of this before?" she muttered as she switched on the light and opened her book. "It's the first time I've been comfortable all day."

The combination of darkness and quiet, the soft bed, the dull book and the fact that she'd been up even earlier than usual that morning was a potent one. Much later, Emily vaguely felt the RV rock as the crew climbed back aboard, and the thought drifted through her mind that she really ought to sit up at least. But she didn't.

A little while after that, she was aware of the steady thrumming of the RV's engine, the hiss of its tires against the highway and a soft rocking motion, which only made her snuggle even more deeply into the pillows. And as the luxurious softness of a blanket was draped over her and the reading light clicked off, she relaxed in the darkness with a contented little sigh.

She didn't know what woke her—silence, perhaps, or lack of motion. For a moment she thought she was in her own bed, somewhere in the dark minutes before her alarm clock sounded, and she yawned and turned over to check the time. If she could just squeeze out another half hour of sleep...

At least, she tried to turn over. She was blocked from moving by a body that was pressed tightly against her back and an arm that lay heavily across her waist, holding her captive.

Panic, born of sleepy confusion, rose in her throat, and she gave a little whimper, turned her head and looked straight at Quinn.

He opened his eyes, but he didn't move.

"What's going on here?" Emily managed.

"Since I was asleep, I haven't any idea." His voice had a rough edge. "Have I missed anything exciting?"

"What are you doing here?"

"Whose bed do you think this is, anyway?" He stretched, as graceful as a cat.

Emily moved as far away as she could, till her back was against the wall. He was between her and the only exit.

Quinn said, "I'd have kissed you awake when we finished the story except that you appeared to be exhausted and, more to the point, I didn't think I'd look good with a shiner. So, since I needed my sleep, too..."

Emily couldn't deny that. A bit of light was filtering into the RV from somewhere, just enough for her to see that his eyelids looked heavy. She supposed some women would think he looked sexy. "Where are we, anyway?"

Quinn propped himself on an elbow and peered out the window. "In the garage behind the station."

"Why?"

"Because that's where we keep the RV. I can't exactly park it on Quality Hill, you know. Oh, you mean why are we still here? I guess because Ivan and Murray, sensitive guys that they are, didn't think they ought to wake us up. Or possibly they weren't sure we'd appreciate being interrupted."

She caught a glimpse of the lighted dial of his watch. "Quinn, it's after two in the morning!"

"Yeah. I figure we've been here a couple of hours. No wonder they didn't want to wake us. We must have been very sound asleep not even to realize we'd stopped moving."

"Or, according to your alternate explanation," Emily snapped, "we were so absorbed in our own activities that we didn't even notice!"

Quinn laughed. "What a lovely idea. Too bad we missed it." He slid off the bed. "Come on, Sleeping Beauty. Time to go home. Your grandmother is probably pacing the floor."

"Of course she isn't." Emily scrambled her possessions into her backpack.

"Well, it's nice to know *she* trusts me, at least," Quinn murmured.

The night air was cold, and Emily shivered in the breeze as Quinn pulled the door of the garage closed behind them. "I thought this was just a warehouse," she said.

"It used to be. But we needed extra security for the RV so we don't have to unpack all the equipment when we come in at some ungodly hour like this." He carried her backpack to her car. "I'll follow you home."

"That's not necessary."

"But, darling, you're not used to being out in the middle of the night."

She wasn't about to argue. If Quinn wanted to trail her all the way to Brookside, instead of going straight home—had he said something about Quality Hill?—that was his business.

And she had to admit there was something comforting about the steady glow of headlights in her mirrors. He was driving a black Jaguar—just about as far as one could get from a recreational vehicle, she reflected.

The Jaguar pulled into the driveway behind her, but Quinn didn't get out. He waited till she was at the door, and then he waved and drove back the way they had come.

The house was warm and quiet, and her bed was invitingly soft. But Emily was a long while getting to sleep.

Only because that deep nap had taken the edge off her exhaustion, she told herself firmly. If it hadn't been for that couple of hours in the RV, she'd have slept like a baby when she got home—as she always did.

It had nothing to do with Quinn.

EMILY HEARD the tiny click the doorbell always made just before it started to peal, and she peered anxiously over her shoulder at Carrie. "Quinn's here already. Is the catch broken?"

"No, it's just stuck." Carrie gave the necklace another tug. "There, it's secure. Don't fiddle with it, though. I'd hate to see you lose this necklace." She hurried off toward the front door.

"Especially since it's yours," Emily called after her. She took a moment to study the necklace's reflection in the pier glass, the gold glowing dully against the crystal clarity of teardrop-shaped diamonds. The necklace was larger and more elaborate than anything she normally wore, but tonight called for all the glitz and glamour she could muster. There would be plenty of it in the audience tonight, and she needed every bit of extra confidence that looking truly wonderful always added.

She picked up her gloves from the table under the pier glass where she'd tossed them when she'd rushed downstairs to beg Carrie's help with the difficult catch. She was just starting to put them on when a reflection caught her eye.

Carrie came into the parlor, Quinn a step behind her. He stopped in the doorway—abruptly, as if he'd run into an invisible wall.

Emily didn't turn around, but she watched him as she put on her long, black kid gloves. They were the tightly fitted kind with button fastenings at wrist and elbow, and it took patience to work her fingers into position, so she had plenty of time to look him over.

She'd been right about the glitz; Quinn was not wearing a tuxedo, but white tie and tails. He was magnificent, tall and straight and lean, every inch perfect from mirror-polished shoes to sun-streaked hair, which for the first time in Emily's memory was brushed into perfect order.

She finished buttoning her gloves; it took even longer than usual because her fingers were trembling just a little. Her back, bare almost to the waist, had been chilly earlier. Now her spine felt warm, as if not only his gaze rested on that expanse of creamy skin, but his hands, as well.

He didn't say a word. And he didn't move from the doorway.

Emily picked up her tiny evening bag and turned to face him. "Well, aren't you a tailor's dream?" she murmured. Her voice sounded odd to her own ears, strained somehow.

Quinn didn't seem to notice. "Thank you," he said. "You look..."

He paused, and Emily's eyebrows rose fractionally. What on earth, she wondered, required so much thought from Quinn, who was never at a loss for words? Was it the way the sequin trim glittered on the close-fitting bodice of her black dress? Or the sweep of the long skirt, which despite its fullness accentuated every curve? Or perhaps the daring plunge of the neckline?

"Well rested," he finished.

That'll teach you, Emily thought. She'd asked him to tone down the nonsense on the show, and it appeared he'd toned it down off the air, as well. It would be silly to be disappointed because he hadn't paid lavish compliments.

"Are you ready?" he asked. "I'm afraid the car's double-parked, because there was no room in the driveway."

"No room?" Emily handed him her black velvet cape. "Don't tell me you've got a limousine."

"You expected to pull up in front of the Kendrick Hotel in the RV?"

"Not exactly. I suppose we do have an image to maintain. I only meant that the Jaguar would have been quite adequate."

Carrie brushed a soft kiss onto Emily's cheek, careful of her makeup, and fastened the high collar of her cape. "Have a good time, darling."

The limo was long and gleaming and black, and beside the back door waited a uniformed chauffeur to help Emily in.

Quinn sank into the leather seat beside her and sighed. "First time I've relaxed all day," he mumbled, and closed his eyes.

"Did you get the stories done?"

"About an hour ago. That's a nice dress, by the way."

She eyed him warily. The words were ordinary enough, but there was a note in his voice that said much more. And in a limousine big enough to seat eight, he'd planted himself right next to her.

Don't be an idiot, Emily told herself. He'd also left enough room between them to avoid crushing her skirt. That definitely indicated the man wasn't so overcome by desire that he was having trouble thinking clearly! "Gran says you can never go wrong with basic black."

"Men learned that a long time ago."

"Really? Then why is it so difficult to get the average guy into a tux?"

"Don't tell me you're in the habit of settling for average guys. Your grandmother made the dress, didn't she?"

"How did you know?"

"Pure instinct. In its own way, it's as off-the-wall as Brenna's wedding gown. Of course, it's not the sort of thing the ordinary grandmother would want her precious lamb wearing out into the world. But Carrie's a different sort, isn't she?"

Emily laughed. "She used to do costumes for the theater."

"I'm not surprised. Surely not in Kansas City, though."

"No, in New York. My mother's still in Manhattan, but when Gran decided to get out of the fast lane, I came with her."

"To be a support and comfort in her declining years, no doubt." Quinn's voice was dry.

"Gran? Decline? Don't make me laugh. I thought I'd stand a better chance of launching my career in a smaller market than New York."

"And look where you've ended up," Quinn said. "I didn't think to offer you dinner before the auction. Are you hungry?"

"I had a snack. I never eat much on nights like this."

"Neither do I, so I've made arrangements for a late supper afterward."

"And if you're still awake by then, you might even enjoy it."

Quinn opened one eye. "Oh, I'll be fine. I'm only suffering from eyestrain and overwork, not lack of sleep. I had a wonderful rest last night, thank you." His voice was lazy.

Emily bit her lip. She shouldn't read meanings into his words; maybe he'd meant exactly what he'd said. After all, he'd been a perfect gentleman when she'd awakened in his arms.

"Thanks for seeing me home last night," she said stiffly.

The corner of his mouth quirked in a contented smile. "You mean this morning?"

All Emily's good intentions went down the drain. "Look, Quinn," she warned. "One word in public about us spending the night together and I'll—"

"But we didn't."

"That's right, and—"

"It was only part of the night. The best part, of course, but only—"

Emily shrieked and reached for him threateningly.

Quinn hastily put up both hands in self-defense. "All right, I promise not to say a word about how beautiful you are when you first wake up!"

She had to settle for that pledge, incomplete as it was, because just then the limousine drew up in front of the Kendrick Hotel. On the sidewalk under the grand marquee a knot of onlookers stood, pointing and exclaiming at the stream of people arriving for the auction.

Quinn waited for the chauffeur to open the door, but he helped Emily out himself, offered his arm and shortened his step to match hers as they climbed the shallow stairs into the main lobby of Kansas City's oldest and most opulent hotel.

Outside the Grand Ballroom, Whitney Townsend spotted them and hurried over. "We've set aside a room for you." She waved a hand toward a door in the corner. "Someone will come and get you five minutes before the auction starts." She consulted her watch. "Just long enough to check your makeup, Emily. You've got perfect timing."

"Don't I get credit?" Quinn complained. "I brought her, after all."

A young man with a clipboard rushed up with a question, and Whitney gave a helpless little shrug and vanished into the Grand Ballroom.

The room in the corner had obviously been furnished with bridal parties in mind. A dressing table ran the full length of one wall, surmounted by dozens of makeup lights, and the opposite wall held a triple full-length mirror. The wallpaper was pale peach, to provide a flattering reflection no matter what color a woman was wearing.

Emily hung her cape on a rack and turned to the mirror to give her hair a final brushing. She'd left it loose around her shoulders tonight, in a mass of curls, and the breeze outside had disarranged it.

On the dressing table were two white florist's boxes, one long and slender, the other short and square. She handed the smaller box to Quinn and opened the other one; in it lay a long-stemmed crimson rose, its velvety petals barely half-open.

He looked over her shoulder at the long-stemmed rose. "Are you sure that one wasn't meant for me? I could carry it between my teeth."

"If I thought it would keep you quiet, I'd be tempted."

He held up a red-rose boutonniere. "Will you pin this? I'm never any good at these things."

Emily fumbled with the pin, terribly aware of how close she was standing to him. She had braced her forearm against his chest to hold the flower steady against his lapel, and his warmth seemed to enfold her. His breath was stirring the hair at her temple, and the rich scent of the flower was drugging her senses. If she lifted her chin a fraction and looked up at him . . .

"There," she said. Her voice shook just a little.

His hands came to rest at her waist. "How about a kiss for luck before we face the crowd?"

Her eyes widened in shock. Had he read her mind? "Luck?" she managed. "*You've* got stage fright?"

"Not exactly. It just seems like a good idea." He was watching her mouth.

Emily shook her head. "My lipstick."

"Don't worry, I won't disturb it. There are all kinds of kisses, you know." He bent his head and his lips softly brushed the sensitive triangle just under her ear.

His mouth was warm. How, then, Emily wondered, could the contact send icy shivers all the way down her spine?

He smiled at her. "That should get us both in the proper mood, don't you think?"

A knock sounded on the door. "Mr. Randolph? Miss Lambert? It's time. I have to get your microphones on."

Unhurried, Quinn released Emily, gently patted her hair into place and handed her the long-stemmed rose. "Ready?"

"I'm afraid I've just come down with a dreadful illness," Emily muttered.

"You wouldn't dream of backing out now. Admit it, you're already thinking up a way to get your revenge in public."

"You did that just to get me off balance, didn't you?" She saw the mischievous smile start to dawn in his eyes and added hastily, "Well, it didn't work."

"You're right," Quinn murmured. "Of course it didn't."

She glared at him, but he didn't say another word except to test his microphone. And as they followed the young man with the clipboard across the mezzanine to the Grand Ballroom, Quinn took her hand comfortingly in his.

As if I needed reassurance, Emily thought.

Despite the sound-deadening effect of the velvet curtain that blocked the arched doorway, she could hear Whitney in the ballroom, launching into an introduction as flattering as any she'd ever heard.

The young man consulted his clipboard. "You'll go in together, past the tables of items and directly up to the small table in front. The runners will bring the items in turn up to the table to be sold. Each item has a tag with full description and target price, and I'll be just offstage with the list if there's any question. There, you're on."

Emily took a deep breath, and they stepped through the curtain. She realized just a moment too late that Quinn was still holding her hand.

The Grand Ballroom was set up as if for a banquet, with rows of round tables, each seating a dozen people. A low stage at one side of the room held a line of tables stacked with items to be auctioned. The chandeliers had been dimmed a bit, so the stage was brighter than the rest of the ballroom, but the spotlights weren't blinding, and it was possible from the stage to see every face—and more important, every upraised hand once the auction started.

Emily looked at the array of merchandise with foreboding; from the look of those loaded tables, they would be here all night.

Applause filled the room, and as they reached center stage it showed no signs of dying. That was the most awkward time of any public appearance, Emily always thought—the brief moments spent standing in front of a crowd with nothing to do but shift from one foot to the other and think how awful it would be to fall on one's face.

But the moment passed, and the applause died down. "I hope you all brought plenty of money," Quinn said. "We've got a lot of wonderful things to sell tonight, don't we?" He turned to Emily and flung one hand up in front of his eyes as if he'd been blinded by the spotlights reflecting in the diamonds at her throat. "I need my sunglasses. Is that necklace real?"

"It certainly isn't imaginary," Emily said sweetly. "And it's not part of the auction loot, so don't get dollar signs in your eyes."

"Did you decide to donate something, after all? I did."

"Don't tell me—it's a videocassette of the best moments of the Traveling Man."

"How'd you guess?"

"A very short cassette, no doubt," Emily murmured.

Quinn looked wounded, but Emily caught the sparkle in his eyes, which the audience couldn't see. She had risen to the challenge, and he was delighted.

"And speaking of making things short," she went on, "let's get started, shall we?"

Quinn turned to the audience. "She can't wait to be alone with me after the show."

Plainly, the evening was going to be like walking a tightrope across Grand Canyon without a safety net. Emily could feel the energy surging through Quinn like a magnetic field, and she knew she could either huddle on the edge and quiver, or she could throw caution to the wind, put her chin up and live dangerously right along with him.

So she lifted the long-stemmed rose to his face and drew the velvety petals down his cheek. "Or maybe, after everything else is sold, I'll donate you to the cause."

Quinn smiled. "Don't, darling. There'd be so much competition it would cost you a fortune to buy me back."

Emily's only answer was a dubious look.

In the meantime, one of the runners had brought the first item to the table, and Emily read the tag, then displayed the bottle of champagne it was attached to, and the auction officially began.

The champagne brought more than the target price, and the woman who bought it gave Quinn an enthusiastic hug. As the buyer returned to her seat, Quinn looked at Emily. "See? It wasn't really the champagne she wanted, it was the hug. I told you there'd be competition if you put me up for sale."

"Who says I even intend to bid?" She launched into the description of the next item.

The special Royals baseball sold for a premium, as did lunch with the mayor. And by the time the tickets and backstage passes for the rock concert came up for sale, the reckless mood on stage seemed to have infected the entire audience.

"The Hunter Dix concert," Emily said, fanning the tickets like a poker hand.

Quinn paused for a drink of water; he was beginning to sound a little hoarse. "I understand the concert is sold out, so these are the last two tickets available in all of Kansas City."

"Probably the scalpers have a few."

"Oh, of course. The last I heard they were asking two hundred dollars each. But if you want a sure seat, this is your last chance."

Emily looked at the tickets pensively, studying the handsome face of the singer printed on each stub. "It's no wonder the tickets were snapped up, Quinn. Hunter Dix is the sexiest man in the world."

The audience gave a sympathetic groan.

"You *are* going to put me up for sale, aren't you?" Quinn accused. "Heartless wench."

A lock of his hair was drooping over his forehead. Emily smoothed it into place. "Don't fret. I'm sure someone will give you a good home."

The bidding for the tickets started briskly. Emily stood quietly on the sidelines for a while, then stepped forward and made a bid of her own.

Quinn paused. Silence settled over the ballroom for ten seconds while he eyed her speculatively. "All right," he said finally. "Your money is as good as anyone else's." He took another bid from the floor and looked at Emily.

She nodded. "Four hundred for the pair."

"That's exactly what the scalpers are getting for ordinary seats, with no backstage passes. Come on, Emily—this is such a good cause, you surely aren't going to be cheap. Tell you what—I'll give five hundred for them myself."

"Why? Quinn, you don't want these tickets."

"You're certain of that?" A half-dozen bids from the floor drove the price up another two hundred dollars before he looked at Emily again.

"Seven-fifty," she said.

"Eight hundred. I'll be a gentleman and take you. We'll make it a real date."

The audience seemed to like that idea; half a dozen women at a front table sighed appreciatively.

Emily raised an eyebrow. "What makes you think I want you to go with me? Eight-fifty."

"Well, in that case, I'm dropping out of the bidding. Who are you taking?"

The bids from the floor went well over a thousand dollars before Emily had a chance to answer. "Thirteen hundred,'' she broke in finally, ''and if you think I'm going to tell you who I'm inviting—''

''Taking the Fifth Amendment, are you?''

''Of course not.''

Quinn laughed. ''It's me,'' he told the audience. ''I'm certain of it. She's just too shy to admit it in public.'' The bidding surged on. Finally he turned to Emily. ''You've been awfully quiet lately.''

''I'm over my budget,'' she admitted.

''Well, there's one last chance. If we'd add our final bids together we'd have twenty-one hundred dollars, and—''

''Twenty-two!'' a woman called from the floor, and Quinn shrugged and sold the package to her. ''What's so special about Hunter Dix?'' he asked when she came to the stage to claim her tickets.

The woman smiled. ''Ask Emily.''

The pair of tickets had been the last item of real value, and the bids on the remaining lots went quickly. But when the last bit of merchandise was sold, a feminine chant started softly at the back of the auditorium—Quinn's name, over and over.

''My faithful fans,'' Quinn said with a sentimental sigh.

Emily shaded her eyes and looked over the crowd. ''You want to know if he's for sale, right?''

There was a roar of agreement.

Emily thought it over. ''I don't believe I'll sell him, after all, because—''

Quinn grinned. ''I knew you wouldn't do it.''

She ignored the interruption. ''It would break his heart if he went cheap.''

''And she only has thirteen hundred dollars to buy me back.''

''Besides, if I can't have Hunter Dix—'' Emily shrugged theatrically ''—I guess I've got no choice but to settle for

Quinn." She tucked her hand through his arm. "Time to go."

For once, Quinn didn't hold out for the last word. He didn't need to; the suggestive lift of his eyebrows as he followed her offstage was every bit as effective.

The limo was waiting at the front of the hotel. Emily sank into the deep leather seat and fanned her face. "That was the most bizarre evening of my life," she accused.

"Don't blame me for all of it." Quinn settled beside her, and the car slid neatly into traffic. "I have one question."

"I know—what's so special about Hunter Dix. Well, it's hard to explain, but he's—"

Quinn shook his head. "I've heard all I care to about him. I want to know if you've got any further reason for saving that lipstick. No? Good." His arm went around her shoulders.

Emily's breath suddenly stuck in her throat. She opened her mouth to protest, but the words wouldn't come.

"I've been waiting all evening to do this," Quinn said against her lips. "If you'd thought to donate a kiss tonight—"

"You'd have bid a dollar or two?"

He whispered, "I wouldn't have stopped at any amount of money, Emily."

And very softly his mouth came to rest on hers.

CHAPTER SEVEN

EMILY HAD BEEN KISSED in the back of a limousine once before—on the night of her senior prom—but she had no illusions that this kiss would be anything like the previous one.

She was right. Quinn's lips were tender and firm, moving slowly and sensually from her mouth to her temple to her chin, neither beseeching nor demanding, and yet the sheer power of his touch was enough to paralyze her. Her mind was spinning as if she'd had too much champagne, and she didn't seem to have the strength to hold her head up, so she let it fall back against the leather seat, and Quinn's mouth traced a line across her throat and came to rest against the throbbing pulse point at the base of her neck. His hands were warm against her spine, under the soft velvet of her cloak, cradling her close—and just how had he managed to get into that position, without her even noticing?

She opened her eyes; it took effort to raise her head, and more willpower not to lift her hand to caress his soft, sun-streaked hair. . . .

He kissed the corner of her mouth, and then just looked at her, not moving, his gaze roving over her face in the dim and shifting light. "Your eyes *are* like brown velvet, just as that magazine reporter said." He sounded surprised, and even a little breathless. "I wonder how he knew."

Emily's voice was little more than a whisper. "Well, I didn't kiss him, if that's what you're wondering."

"Mmm. I'm glad."

His breath tickled her cheek, and before Emily realized what she was doing, she had turned her head to seek his mouth again. He might have been waiting all evening for this opportunity, but she had been waiting much longer than that. The tension between them had been building all week toward this inevitable moment.

Last night, when they had awakened together in the RV and she had almost panicked, she had thought for a moment that she was afraid of him. But that hadn't been the problem at all. Her own reactions had been the source of her fear. He was so very attractive, so very desirable, and the fact that he seemed to feel the same way about her certainly didn't diminish the power of her response. . . .

The limousine slid to a halt so smooth it was almost imperceptible. The chauffeur didn't move or speak.

Slowly Quinn pulled away, his hands lingering on the small of Emily's back. "I should have told him to take the long way around," he said ruefully. "Can't think why I didn't—unless your perfume is fogging my brain."

Emily frowned a little. "I'm not wearing any."

"I know. You don't need the kind they sell in stores."

But she hardly heard him. She glanced out the window, remembering what he'd said earlier about a late supper after the auction was over. But there was no restaurant in sight, and they had not stopped in the bustle of a commercial district. This was a much quieter neighborhood, one of the older areas of Kansas City, now being rebuilt with expensive new town houses and apartment complexes. Quinn had brought her to Quality Hill.

Ending up alone at his place was not a good idea, she thought. Not when the situation was as combustible as this.

But perhaps she was jumping to conclusions. She wasn't really familiar with Quality Hill, but somewhere she had read that part of the charm of the redevelopment was a neighborhood atmosphere with plenty of services available. That might well include a quiet little restaurant that would happily provide a private supper for two people in no mood to face crowds. Then again, she still didn't see any commercial signs....

"Your place?" she said finally.

"My town house. I didn't think another public appearance was quite in order." His voice was playful. "Especially since by now I'm probably wearing whatever's left of your lipstick."

Emily didn't answer. She didn't look at him, either. She told herself she must have imagined the breathlessness she'd thought she heard in his voice a few moments ago.

"So after the chauffeur left us at the hotel, he stopped at the caterer's to pick up a basket, and here we are. Peace, quiet and Maine lobster with drawn butter. The perfect end to the evening, wouldn't you say?"

Emily bit the tip of her tongue. There was absolutely nothing out of line about his plans. A pleasant, private, relaxing little supper, shared after a job well done. It was very thoughtful of him, actually.

But for a moment, she had forgotten that this was simply the last act of the charity auction. For a moment, she had wanted it to be more.

The idea left her feeling chilly, as if the cold wind had invaded the car, swirled under her velvet cape and caressed her bare spine, where Quinn's hands had rested only moments before.

Emily said abruptly, "I don't think this is such a good idea."

She thought he hesitated, but she couldn't have sworn to it. "Being alone, you mean? Listen, Emily, that was a kiss, not a proposition." He sounded annoyed.

Emily didn't blame him. He had no way of knowing that the game he was enjoying so much was affecting her in an entirely different way. And she wasn't about to come straight out and tell him she was in danger of forgetting that this was only an act.

She ought to just take a deep breath and go inside his house and enjoy a wonderful supper and his company and a bit more flirtation. But she simply couldn't—not till she'd had a chance to get a grip on herself once more.

She let her eyebrows arch delicately. "I only meant that I'm very tired and I'd like to go home."

He looked at her for a long moment, then leaned forward and pushed the intercom button to tell the driver to take them to Brookside. There was a rough edge to his tone as he gave the order.

"You've strained your voice," Emily said. "It would probably be better if you rested it, anyway."

"No doubt," Quinn said crisply. "I'll give you credit, though. That's the most polite way I've ever been told to shut up."

Emily bit her lip. "That wasn't what I meant."

"It sounded like it. Dammit, Emily, if I didn't ravish you last night when I found you in my own bed, I hardly think I'd be overcome by temptation now."

He was right; the situation last night had been every bit as ripe for trouble as this one, and he'd behaved like a perfect gentleman. The difference was in Emily herself. She'd been dismayed last night, but not rattled like this.

She managed a note of amusement. "I know better than to think you have designs on me, Quinn. Believe me, I'm just tired."

Quinn settled back into the corner of the limousine with a sigh, as if he was relieved.

The house in Brookside was dark except for a speck of light in the kitchen when the limousine stopped in the street. Quinn opened the door before the chauffeur could move from his seat and offered Emily his hand as if he half expected her to slap it away.

She didn't, so he tucked her arm through his and walked her to the back door. He stopped on the steps and looked down at her. The wind ruffled his hair a little, and the streetlights cast a silvery glow across his face. "Maybe you're right," he said. "It wasn't such a good idea." His lips brushed her forehead, so lightly it was like the kiss of a falling leaf. Then he took two steps down the sidewalk and stopped. "Emily?"

She turned with her hand on the doorknob.

"Want some lobster? I've got plenty."

She was relieved that the playful note was back in his voice once more. At least he wasn't looking for hidden meanings anymore. She smiled and shook her head. "See you Monday, Quinn."

He gave her a little salute as he climbed into the car.

Emily was still smiling as she pushed the door shut behind her. Quinn was one of a kind, that was sure. He was like a tennis ball that hadn't passed factory inspection—one never knew which way he'd bounce next.

That wasn't a bad comparison. It might come in handy next week on the show, and it was bound to get a laugh. . . .

"Did you have a good time?" Carrie asked.

Emily was startled; she hadn't seen her grandmother standing in the dim kitchen with a teacup in one hand. "It was . . . interesting."

"Why didn't you invite Quinn in. It's cold."

Emily started unbuttoning her gloves. "Because I'm awfully tired. Were you waiting up for me?"

"Certainly not," Carrie said acidly. "When did I ever?"

"Well, I thought you'd stopped when I turned twenty-one."

"I was waiting up for my necklace." Carrie held out a hand, palm up.

Emily laughed, draped her cape over the back of a chair and released the catch at the back of her neck. The soft brush of warm gold against the skin right under her ear reminded her of the way Quinn had kissed her just before the auction started. That had been planned for effect, too, of course, to add sparks to the show. She couldn't exactly blame him for turning up the flame under the stew they'd created. She would just have to keep reminding herself that there was nothing more to it than that.

"I like him, Emily."

Emily folded her cape carefully over her arm and said thoughtfully, "So do I. Good night, Gran."

Tired though she was, Emily was too keyed up to feel sleepy. She hung up her dress, then took off her makeup and mixed a ghastly green facial mask which she applied to her cheeks, chin and forehead. Finally she turned off the lights, lighted the gas log in the fireplace in her room and settled into the armchair beside it.

It was sheer luxury to be sitting by the fire, wrapped in the most comfortable bathrobe she owned, her feet relaxing in quilted slippers that were a couple of sizes too big. Nobody who had been at the Kendrick Hotel this evening would recognize her now, that was sure. She would have smiled at the thought, except that the facial mask was already tightening and she couldn't.

She wondered what Quinn would have said about the mask if she'd been wearing it last night in the RV. He'd probably have screamed and run—except in that confined area there was nowhere to run to.

She frowned. What had he said once about not living in the RV except when he had to? She hadn't paid much attention at the time, but she understood his feelings now that she'd had some experience with the RV's limited space.

At least his bed had been pleasantly cozy. That would help make the situation more bearable if he and his crew were on the road for days at a time. She wondered if the bunks were as comfortable. Probably not; they couldn't be much wider than a cot. Besides, if the table had to be folded away in order to reveal the beds, just getting ready to sleep would be a major undertaking. No wonder Quinn had simply curled up with her last night.

How did the three of them manage, anyway, when they were on the road for long periods of time? They must have developed a wonderful relationship—or incredible self-discipline—to avoid quarrels and petty resentments. Or perhaps they were all just little boys at heart, more interested in adventure than creature comforts.

Though Quinn certainly seemed to appreciate the finer things. Limousines and lobster, white ties and town houses. He had seemed even more at ease with those than in the RV.

She stared at the fire for a long time. What if Quinn wasn't as happy as the Traveling Man as she'd assumed he was? Until now, Emily had discounted what he'd said about the discomforts; every job had its downside, and it was no wonder he was grumpy, with his duties abruptly doubled. But what if he'd really meant that he was tired of the job altogether?

Why had he deliberately set out to shake up the whole framework of "Kansas City Morning"? She had thought he was trying to push Jason Manning into relieving him of the responsibility. But what if Quinn, like Brad Jarrett, expected that Gary wouldn't be coming back and anticipated that a permanent slot on "Kansas City Morning" might be available soon?

Was it possible that it wasn't the show he disliked, only the double duty? If he had his choice between the two, might he even prefer hosting "Kansas City Morning" to being the Traveling Man?

Brad had been quite open about his ambitions. The fact that Quinn had stayed quiet didn't mean he didn't see things the same way. And Quinn had a big advantage in that he was already on the spot, rather than trying to break in as Brad was doing. He could demolish the rules and actually demonstrate what a morning show could be, if he was in charge.

He had already expanded the set, invited the studio audience and lengthened and deepened the interviews. All these things, which she'd thought he was doing in an effort to be kicked off the show, could have been a deliberate attempt to draw attention, and viewers, and higher ratings. That was precisely what had happened, after all.

And as for the chemical magic he had created with his cohost—the magic that had the viewers tuning in and speculating what would happen next—of course that had been deliberate, too. And as for being effective, Emily could almost hear the questions. When would he kiss her on the air? Would she go to bed with him? Or had she already done so but hadn't admitted it yet?

She'd always known he was encouraging that speculation. If she let herself believe, however, that the sparks between them were anything more than illusion, she was truly a fool.

She didn't doubt that Quinn found her attractive. Brad Jarrett was coldhearted enough to make up to any woman who might be able to give his career a boost; Quinn wasn't. But it was equally silly to think he found her irresistible.

He'd never even made a move to get acquainted before "Kansas City Morning" had come up for grabs.

This was a job, after all, and the byplay between them was simply a part of it. He'd said as much yesterday when she'd asked him to tone things down and he'd refused. The fact that they liked each other added to the spice, of course, but it didn't mean there was anything serious going on.

They were two professionals, brought together by accident for a short time; there was nothing more to it than that. Their job was to entertain, and if they had fun along the way, who could possibly object? That was Quinn's philosophy, and for Emily's sake, it had better be hers, as well.

She washed off the mask, turned off the gas fire and in the subdued darkness of her room pulled the blankets up to her chin.

It's all right to like him, Emily, she told herself. It's all right to play along. Just don't let yourself believe any of it is real.

MONDAY'S LIVE AUDIENCE was the biggest yet, and Tish was at the back of the studio, trying to shoo people to their seats when Emily came in. "This is impossible," the director said from between gritted teeth. "They're still coming in."

Emily shrugged. "Maybe we'll have to make a rule that any seat not taken half an hour before the show stays vacant."

Tish shot her a look. "It was a whole lot easier when *all* the seats were vacant!"

Emily didn't bother to argue. She glanced at the studio clock. It was still five minutes to airtime, but Quinn was already on the set, lounging in one of the tall chairs at center stage and talking to the people in the front row. He saw her come in and lifted a hand in lazy greeting.

Emily's heartbeat sped up. There was no reason to feel skittish, but she wasn't eager to join him any earlier than necessary. Five minutes could be an eternity when there was nothing to say.

So she worked her way slowly down the ramp toward the set, greeting audience members, shaking hands, signing bits of paper. One young woman pressed a photograph of a baby into her hand. A very young man shyly offered her a flower—a single daffodil, which Emily tucked into the belt loop of her skirt. An older woman occupying an aisle seat and crocheting something large and garish smiled pleasantly. Emily paused beside her, but the woman didn't put her work down long enough for a handshake. Three men in business suits, sitting in a row near the front and talking to each other, almost ignored her.

It was a strange mix of an audience.

Quinn rose as she reached the set and offered a hand to help her into her chair. He eyed the daffodil. "Taking flowers from other men, hmm?"

Emily touched the silky flower with a fingertip. "He was a dear to bring it." She folded her hand around the tiny microphone on the lapel of her silk blouse to block it. She knew that the faster she launched their usual banter, the easier it would be, but she didn't feel quite comfortable letting the audience listen in just yet. "I'm sorry about Saturday night, Quinn."

Quinn's eyebrows rose. "You are?"

She could feel a tinge of color creeping up into her cheeks. "Yes," she said lightly. "I've been craving lobster ever since."

Quinn threw back his head and laughed heartily just as the control room cued the start of the show and the camera's red light winked on.

That's great, she thought. We go on the air with Quinn laughing like a hyena...

And incidentally making her look like the most fascinating female in the world. Well, what woman could object to that?

"You wore my skirt," Quinn was saying with satisfaction.

"*Your* skirt?" Emily smoothed one hand over the off-white linen and looked innocently at the audience. "Tell me, what kind of accessories do you wear with it?"

"You know what I mean. It's not mine, exactly. It's the skirt I chose for you the day we went shopping at... I'm only getting myself in deeper, aren't I?"

Emily nodded.

"Can we start over again?"

"It's live TV, Quinn," she explained patiently, as if he were a child. "It's not like videotape, where you can keep on doing takes till you get it right."

"Sometimes that's a lot of fun. Depending on the activity, of course. Why are you turning pink, Emily? Should we talk about the celebrity auction Saturday night, instead?" He turned to the audience and said firmly, "This was not a date, you remember."

There was scattered laughter in the studio.

"No, I mean it," Quinn insisted. "I won't say that we didn't have fun while we worked—"

"A bit," Emily admitted.

"As fund-raisers go, that one was the most interesting ever. Of course, I understand that you're still broken-hearted over not getting the tickets to the Hunter Dix concert, but..."

From the corner of her eye, Emily caught a stealthy movement behind Quinn, at the very edge of the set. She turned her head a fraction to get a better look. Brad Jarrett was spreading papers over the surface of a small table, one Gary used frequently for interviews.

What in heaven's name was Brad doing in the studio when he was supposed to be down in the newsroom waiting for his cue? And what could she do about it, now that they were actually live on the air?

She shot a look at Quinn, who was chatting comfortably about concerts and celebrities and fund-raisers in general. He couldn't see Brad, she realized, and had no idea what was going on behind his back.

"...a nonparty," Quinn was saying. "I think it's a terrific idea and makes a lot of sense for busy people today. The organizers sell tickets as they would for any fund-raiser, but instead of having to dress up and go out for an evening, people get to stay home and put on their jammies and do whatever they like."

"Next you'll think up the non-costume ball," Emily said almost at random. She was still watching Brad, who had settled himself in a chair and was sorting papers into stacks. What was worse, a good part of the audience was watching him, too.

Quinn smiled. "In which sense do you mean that, Emily?"

Tish was having a fit in the control room. Emily knew the moment that Quinn spotted her gyrations, because a tiny wrinkle appeared between his eyebrows. Obviously he didn't understand what Tish was trying to tell him; Emily wouldn't have had a clue, either, if she didn't know what was going on at the far side of the set.

Tish threw up her hands and started over. First a shake of her head, then a slitting motion across her throat, then a finger pointed toward Brad.

Don't cut to him, Emily interpreted. She nodded slightly, and relief flooded over Tish's face.

"I mean no costumes," Emily explained. "People could wear signs to identify the character they're portraying. Think of the savings in effort, to say nothing of costs."

"And here I thought you meant there'd be no clothes involved at all." Quinn took a folded slip of paper from his breast pocket. "As we promised last week, we have the rules for the Name Baby Wright contest, to be followed by the news."

Emily pretended to flick a speck of lint off her collar and blocked her microphone long enough to mutter, "No news."

"What?"

Emily gritted her teeth. "Don't ask stupid questions, Quinn. *No news.*" She uncovered the microphone. "Tell us about the contest rules."

Quinn shook out his paper and cleared his throat. "Everyone knows what an impact a name has on a person's self-image and life success. There have even been studies showing that Michael and Jennifer get better grades than Cecil and Winnifred do—no matter how smart they all actually are. So I want everyone to take this very seriously."

Emily leaned back in her chair and fanned herself languidly. "I can hardly wait to hear your suggestions."

"Really? I do have a few examples here, of course, and I'm flattered that you want me to share them. For instance, if Robin would like him—"

"Or her," Emily interposed.

"That goes without saying. My suggestion is a gender-neutral name."

"I'm proud of you, Quinn. I think."

"If she wants to end up with a Supreme Court justice, she can call the baby Constitutional Wright."

Emily groaned.

"Or if she prefers to promote a military career—"

"Don't tell me."

Quinn was not deterred. "Right Left Wright. And if it should be a girl and homemaking is the goal—of course, you can call me sexist here—"

"I no doubt will," she said dryly.

"We could name her Looking for Mister Wright."

"Oh, Quinn!"

He grinned. "Well, you've got the idea. Send in your nominations for Robin's baby's name to the station, and we'll announce the best ones right here."

In the control room, Tish was signaling an order for an advertising break; Emily cut in smoothly and announced the commercial. As soon as the camera flicked off, Quinn said, "What do you mean, no news? Did someone blow up the newsroom?"

"In a manner of speaking, yes." Emily tipped her head toward the table where Brad sat. "Welcome to the real world of live television."

He sighed. "I'm going on strike for videotape."

The studio audience was enthralled. Tish had stormed out of the control room and across the set and was standing over Brad, arms akimbo. She spoke quietly, so Emily couldn't catch the words, but the fury in her tone came across clearly nevertheless.

Brad, on the other hand, made no effort to keep his voice low. "Giving up the fake skyline background in the newsroom is little enough sacrifice for the sake of a unified presentation," he said. "This way we're all part of a single team, pulling together to create the best program for—"

"Part of a *team?*" Tish shrieked. "If I could fire you, Brad, you'd be gone!"

"That's beside the point, isn't it? Is there going to be a newscast this morning or not? There isn't time for me to get back to the newsroom, and there's no one else down there. So I read the news from here or we do without."

Tish tugged at her bottom lip. Obviously, Emily thought, the director didn't need to be told that the morning news was a requirement for the station's license, and eliminating it was a violation of law. "You do it from here," Tish said finally. "And if you show your face on this set again, Brad Jarrett—"

"You can't fire me. You said so yourself."

"No. But I'll spray you with Mace till you'll wish you'd only been fired!" She retreated to the control room.

The break was ending, and one of the cameras wheeled around to focus on Brad. To Emily's relief, he played the news straight—his voice deep and convincing, his manner professional and serious. And though he stayed on the set through the rest of the show, he didn't intrude until the final moments, and then he simply came across the stage to join Quinn and Emily as they waved goodbye.

It was the first time Emily realized it was possible to bite one's tongue and smile at the same time.

As soon as the camera went dark, she wheeled around and jabbed a finger into Brad's tie. "We've got some things to talk about," she stormed.

He grinned. "Sure. Tish backed down in a hurry when I asserted myself, didn't she?"

Quinn unclipped Emily's microphone. "Come on, let's get out of here. It wouldn't do your image any good to hit him when the public can see."

She had to admit the sense of that. Once outside the studio, though, she turned on Brad. "Dammit, what were you trying to accomplish?"

Brad shrugged. "Well, since Tish doesn't approve of the live audience, she's never had the monitors properly set up in the studio, which means the people here can't see the news. So I moved."

"Why on earth you think that's an answer..." Emily's voice failed.

Quinn leaned against the wall and stuck both hands in his trouser pockets. "What gives, Brad?" he asked easily.

"I got a tip there'd be VIPs in the audience today. Network people. Talent scouts, if you want to call them that."

"Checking us out?" Emily gasped, and recalled the three guys in the business suits who looked like they didn't belong. Of all the days for the show to fall apart under their feet. "I really appreciate getting a warning, Brad," she said dryly.

"I would have told you before the show," he said defensively, "but I didn't have time."

"Don't worry about it, Emily," Quinn said. "I can think of a thousand reasons network people would stop by, but none of them involve looking for new talent."

"You sound awfully sure of that," Brad challenged.

"I am. What network bigwig's got time to chase across the country hunting for rising stars? They all get more sample tapes of promising performers than they can possibly view." He smiled at Emily. "Besides, Brad's never right about anything important. They were probably exterminators, and he just heard wrong."

She couldn't help laughing.

Brad's face reddened, and he stalked off down the hall toward the newsroom.

"I almost wish he *would* get discovered," Quinn said thoughtfully. He pushed himself away from the wall and strolled toward the dressing rooms. "Things would be a whole lot more peaceful around here if it wasn't for Brad."

Emily dropped into step beside him. "Maybe Tish will edit a sample tape of his best stuff, and we can send it in."

They were passing the director's office just then. The door was open and Tish's back was to it. She was holding the telephone quite a distance from her ear.

The reason was obvious; even from outside the room, Emily could hear the voice on the other end of the line. She recognized it, too, and she knew what must have happened. Over in the hospital, someone had slipped up and given Gary Bennington a television set.

CHAPTER EIGHT

As IF SHE SENSED their presence, Tish turned around, with the telephone still a good eight inches from her ear, and sat down on the corner of her desk.

"Sorry," Emily whispered.

Tish cupped a hand over the mouthpiece. "What?"

"Gary wasn't supposed to have a television. I'd arranged it, or at least I thought I had."

"His wife took him a portable set this morning."

"Of all the days for him to see the show..."

Tish shrugged. "It wasn't that much worse than usual."

Emily winced.

"Gary's wife always was a bit dense," Tish went on. "Or maybe she hasn't had a chance to see the show herself, so she didn't realize what Gary was likely to think. Well, it's done now."

"Is he having another heart attack or something?"

"Actually it sounds more like a stroke this time."

Emily's eyes widened.

"Not really." Tish smiled, but her eyes looked strained. "I'm just indulging in a bit of tasteless black humor." She put the telephone back to her ear. "Emily's right here," she said cheerfully. "Do you want to talk to her?"

Emily shook her head violently.

Quinn, who was leaning against the door frame with his arms folded across his chest, murmured, "I never thought you were chicken, Emily. Gary can't bite you from a mile away."

Tish was holding out the telephone. Emily, feeling deserted on all sides, took it gingerly.

Gary didn't bother with greetings or amenities. "What the hell are you letting him do to my show?" he snapped.

Quinn took his jacket off and sat down on the arm of a chair as if he expected to be there for some time.

"*Letting* him? Just try stopping him!" But she felt a tiny flare of relief; at least Gary wasn't blaming her.

"Passing the buck, Emily, darling?" Quinn murmured.

Emily glared at him and cupped a hand over the mouthpiece. "Merely giving credit where it's due," she said sweetly. She turned back to Gary. "Quinn's completely unmanageable."

"Quinn?" He sounded surprised. "Oh, nobody expects anything sensible from Quinn. He snapped long ago. But that idiot Brad..."

Emily swallowed hard. "You're more worried about Brad than Quinn?"

Quinn held out both hands, palms up, as if to say, *Didn't I tell you?*

She broke into Gary's list of complaints. "I don't think Brad will cause any further disruption as long as there aren't more talent scouts in the audience."

Gary snorted. "After what they saw this morning, I don't think that will be a problem!"

"No doubt you're right," Emily said. She handed the telephone back to Tish.

Quinn stood up. "You look as if you need to get away."

"Good idea." Emily noticed that her fingers were still trembling. "What have you got in mind? You wouldn't happen to be interviewing a cowboy somewhere in west Texas today?"

"West Texas? We couldn't be back in time for the show tomorrow."

"Does it matter?"

Quinn smothered a grin. "What I had in mind, actually, was brunch. There's still some lobster."

"I'll take it."

Emily didn't bother to change clothes. She grabbed her purse, her backpack, and the new books and briefing notes Jason's secretary had left in her dressing room during the show. She didn't even look at the stack. The sooner she got out of the station the better, for the moment Gary finished chewing up Tish, he was likely to call Jason Manning, and then anything might happen.

"You realize we may not have a show at all by tomorrow?" she told Quinn as he solicitously tucked her into the Jaguar.

"What? I wasn't listening, I'm afraid. I was watching that intriguing slit in your skirt. Didn't I tell you it was a good choice?"

"I'll return it to the store this afternoon," Emily said acidly.

"And they can put it in the window as a museum display. What a novel idea!"

"Dammit, Quinn, will you be serious? What if Gary makes Jason fire us?"

"He can't." He walked around the car and slid behind the wheel.

"Gary's got a contract."

Quinn nodded. "It's airtight and gives him a lot of power, yes, and it has three years to run. But—"

"Three? I thought it was shorter than that." Jason had implied that Gary would retire in a couple of years, maybe even sooner.

"But Jason owns the show," Quinn finished.

Emily bit her lower lip while she thought about it. It was common knowledge that Gary's audience was an aging one, while a younger crowd of viewers, with plenty of disposable income, would attract different sorts of advertisers and induce them to pay more for the privilege of sponsoring "Kansas City Morning." That was no surprise to Emily; it was, after all, the main reason Jason Manning had given for hiring her. But all those plans had been for the future—after Gary retired. If Jason intended to seize this opportunity to change things now, to force Gary out...

"So that means..." she said slowly. "You don't suppose Jason wants Gary to quit before his contract is completed?"

"The idea had occurred to me."

"Then why doesn't he just offer to buy Gary out?"

Quinn shrugged. "It's a very expensive contract."

"So Jason's trying to force the issue? But that's..."

"Nasty? Yes, a bit. But when you're riding the ratings, honey, you don't stop to be a good guy."

"I would," Emily said.

"I know you would. You're too tenderhearted for your own good, Emily. They'll eat you alive in this industry if you aren't careful." He reached over and tousled her hair. "Don't ever let yourself believe that Jason doesn't have his eye on the bottom line—no matter who pays in the end."

Emily was still mulling over that when the Jaguar stopped in front of Quinn's town house. "If you'd be more comfortable," he said, "we can pack up our brunch and take it to the park."

She shifted position just enough to hold up one foot and display the slender high heel of her shoe.

"Nice ankles," Quinn murmured.

"I wasn't fishing for compliments. Does this look like proper garb for a picnic?"

His gaze slid slowly up her body. "Well, now that you mention it... I'll have to make a closer inspection to be certain, of course, but—"

"Never mind the details. Look, Quinn, don't be silly. I wasn't running away Saturday night. I was just tired." It wasn't quite the truth, but maybe close enough. "Let's forget it ever happened, all right?"

"All right," he agreed cheerfully. "It never happened. And if you don't want to go to the park, we'll spread a blanket on the living-room floor and have a picnic right here."

"Trust you to get a blanket in there somewhere!"

The house was surprisingly roomy. Or else, Emily decided as she followed Quinn past a small den and down a hall to the kitchen, perhaps it seemed so large and airy simply because there was so little furniture and so many windows. The living room at the back of the house held only a couch, a couple of chairs, and an oddly angled wall full of electronic gear. Her heels clicked against the hardwood floor, and the cathedral ceiling bounced the sound back to her.

Yet simple as it was, the furniture was obviously carefully chosen and comfortable. Bright-colored rugs divided the expanses of highly polished wood, and a couple of quilts draped the rail of the circular staircase, built of the same golden wood as the floor and rising from a corner of the living room. She suspected that the textiles were the only thing that kept the room from echoing like a public lobby.

She leaned against the tiled counter that divided the kitchen from the living room and watched as Quinn raided the refrigerator and started dumping ingredients in a skillet.

"Can I help?" she offered, but only halfheartedly. It was obvious the man was perfectly competent; anyone who could crack an egg with one hand had spent more time in a kitchen than Emily had.

He waved a hand at a built-in sideboard near the small square dining table. "Place mats and napkins are in the right-hand drawer."

The linens were nice ones, of a nubby natural-colored fiber. "I'm amazed that a minimalist household like this contains place mats," Emily remarked.

"It wouldn't, but my mother gave them to me for Christmas last year. Dishes in that cabinet." He pointed. "And cutlery..." He pulled open a drawer beside him.

Emily set the table with chunky white stoneware. "These are interesting. No two pieces are quite alike."

"Of course not. They were made by an artist in Nebraska."

"I know, you did a story on him."

Quinn smiled. "Her. Couldn't you tell by the sensual feel of the cups?"

"I'm no art critic. The finer details of interpretation go straight over my head." She came back to lean against the counter. "That's starting to smell awfully good."

Quinn stirred the contents of the skillet, then whisked several eggs in a measuring cup and poured them in. "This is what I call the hungry man's lobster soufflé."

Emily looked at the skillet doubtfully. "I don't claim to be a gourmet cook, but that doesn't look like any soufflé I've ever seen."

"Unlike the regular variety, it doesn't take two hours to prepare. Besides, when it comes right down to it, all a soufflé consists of is scrambled eggs and air. I've just left out the air."

"I see your point."

"There's a bottle of white wine in the refrigerator, and glasses on the rack. Hand me the plates, would you?"

By the time they sat down to eat a few minutes later, the savory smell was making Emily light-headed with hunger. "I can see why you're the cook on the road," she said as she shook out her napkin.

"We started out taking turns, but after a couple of days of bologna sandwiches and canned tomato soup, I went on strike." Quinn refilled her wineglass.

Emily buttered a bite of French bread. "How did the stories turn out?"

"Not my prizewinning best."

"But under the circumstances..."

He shrugged. "Quite right. Not every piece can be perfect."

"Especially after... How long have you been doing this? Four years, did you say?"

"No. I've been back in Kansas City that long. I've been at the station about three."

No wonder he was ready for a change. Anyone's imagination would flag after three years of pressure to produce a new, light, upbeat story every single day.

Emily sampled the lobster concoction. The dish was more like an omelet than a soufflé, she decided, but whatever the fine details, it tasted wonderful. "What brought you back here, anyway?"

"My mother was ill."

"Oh. I'm sorry."

"She's fine now, but things were dicey for a while. And since she's not getting any younger, I decided to stay a little closer to home."

"Where were you before?"

"Here and there. You know what it's like in broadcasting—no one stays anywhere forever, Gary Bennington to the contrary."

"Do you really think Jason's trying to get rid of him?"

"How should I know, Emily? Gary's heart attack may make the whole thing a moot question. Or perhaps Jason doesn't have any ulterior motives—he may just be trying to cover all the bases so he doesn't get any nasty surprises."

"I'd much rather think that, instead of looking for a devious plot."

He studied her quizzically. "You *are* a bit sheltered, aren't you?"

"And you're cynical, Quinn Randolph! Why can't a whole production staff work as a team, instead of against each other? What about trust?"

"All right, maybe I'm cynical. But you're not realistic. Don't you even realize that Tish would cut your throat in a minute to save her job?"

Emily nodded. "She's loyal to Gary, and I don't blame her. But that's exactly what's wrong, Quinn. If everyone working on 'Kansas City Morning' really believed that the show was more important than any one member of the team..." Emily tore a slice of French bread into tiny bits. "I can't believe you're arguing against me, not when you've got a wonderful relationship with your own crew."

"Three guys in an RV is a little different from the kind of thing you're talking about. If you ever get the system fixed, Emily, I want to see it in operation." He cleared the plates and poured her coffee. "For dessert, we have an insanely rich cheesecake."

"After that meal, how do you think I could manage another bite?" But she took one look at the dessert he pulled out of the refrigerator and nodded. "Where did you get this?"

Quinn set a slice in front of her. "Brenna brought it over yesterday. It's a bribe."

Emily took a bite. The cheesecake was rich and full-bodied and wonderful. "No matter what Brenna wanted," she said indistinctly, "I hope you told her she could have it."

"One of her ushers had an appendectomy over the weekend, which means he won't be up to performing in her grand opera of a wedding next Saturday, and she needs a replacement."

"Well, that's not too bad, as requests go." She cut another bite and savored it. "Personally, I'd probably rob a bank for this."

"No, you wouldn't. You can buy all you want at a little place down on Country Club Plaza—that's where Brenna got it. But if you want to please her by putting on a tux and filling in for the absent usher, I won't stand in your way. It's a shame your hair's so long, though."

"You mean you're not going to help her out?"

"I said I'd think about it and let her know after I finished the cheesecake."

"What kind of cousin are you?"

"A careful one, when it comes to Brenna. There probably wasn't really an appendectomy at all."

"You're a suspicious beast, Quinn."

"I know Brenna a whole lot better than you do. She's probably had this slot saved for me all along. And no doubt a bridesmaid she thinks would be perfect for me."

"Suspicious *and* heartless."

He feigned shock. "Do you know, Emily, I believe you're right."

"It's a wedding, Quinn. Just because you take part doesn't mean you're eager to embrace the institution. She can't shanghai you into getting married yourself."

"Don't put anything past Brenna. Why don't you come to the wedding and protect me?"

"Because I'm not invited."

"Oh, Brenna wouldn't mind, as long as you promise not to upstage her."

"When she's wearing that dress? Impossible." Emily pushed the last few crumbs of cheesecake around on her plate and reluctantly decided that under no circumstances could she justify eating another piece. "But frankly, even if you needed protection, which I doubt you will, I can't see myself as a bodyguard."

Quinn leaned back in his chair and studied her thoughtfully. "Can't you? It's a very easy job. All you'd have to do is lean on my arm and look fondly up into my eyes, and the average bridesmaid would get over any vain dreams of captivating me."

"If I could pull that off, I'd win an Academy Award hands down." She pushed back her chair. "Let me clean up the mess, at least. You've done all the work."

Quinn didn't argue. Instead of going away, however, as she'd expected he would, he poured himself another cup of coffee and loitered around the kitchen, watching her work. The room was well equipped and efficiently arranged, but it wasn't very big, so Emily kept bumping into him. Every time she touched him, she remembered Saturday night and the kiss in the back of the limousine, and her nerves tightened just a little more.

You're supposed to have forgotten that, she reminded herself. But putting it out of her mind was easier said than done. What would happen if she leaned against him as she reached up to hang the skillet back in place? It would be so easy...

Had he meant that extravagant compliment about the bridesmaids? Of course not, Emily told herself. No woman who cherished daydreams about Quinn would give them up merely because Emily was hanging around, and he was self-assured enough to know it.

She put the last plate in the dishwasher and wiped the sink dry. "Well, that's that," she said lightly. "Thanks for brunch and the break—I feel much better. But I'm sure you have plans for the rest of your day, so. . ."

She was almost disappointed when he didn't deny it, just slid off the counter where he'd been sitting and reached into his pocket for the car keys. "As a matter of fact, I'm going to see a movie. Want to come along?"

"What? Oh, you mean since you worked most of the weekend, you're taking the afternoon off?"

"Not exactly. Remember the actress we're interviewing tomorrow? Her new movie just opened across town, so I'm going to the matinee. Since you always nab the preview tapes, I have to search out other ways to do research."

Emily ignored the accusing note in his voice. "The tape's in my backpack. I picked it up this morning."

Quinn dropped the keys into his pocket. "Then let's watch it here."

As he cued the machine, Emily kicked off her shoes and curled up on one end of the couch. "That wall looks more like a control room than an entertainment center," she observed. There were three tape decks, the home version of theater sound, a wide-screen television and a whole lot of equipment she didn't even recognize. "Do you edit your stories right here?"

"The Traveling Man stuff? Not for broadcast, just my own copies." He came to sit beside her, a remote control in one hand. "And the tape's always cued up so I can show it at the drop of a hat whenever I want to bore someone into leaving early."

"May I see it?"

"Why? Do you want to be bored? It's the equivalent of showing vacation slides."

She drew a little farther into the corner of the couch. "I'd like to see what you think are your best stories."

"We'll see if you still feel that way after the movie." He pushed a button on the remote control, and the light in the room slowly and silently faded as though dusk had fallen outside.

"How did you do that?" Emily craned her neck at the high windows. She could see no shades or curtains, just dark glass.

"Polarization and an electrical current. Nice trick, isn't it?" Another button, and the movie began. Quinn sighed and stretched an arm across the back of the couch, almost around Emily's shoulders. "All the advantages of the theater, with no other people to cause distractions and no messy soda spills on the floor," he mused. "Isn't it great?"

He needn't worry about being distracted, that was true, Emily thought. *He* was the distraction. He didn't move any closer, and his arm didn't even brush her body; he simply settled back and concentrated on the movie. But Emily was aware of every breath he drew and every movement he made. So much for the idea of simply forgetting what had happened in the limousine Saturday night!

The movie was a period piece, full of elegant costumes and swashbuckling actors and rollicking action that somehow never melded together into a convincing whole. "What did you think?" Emily asked when the final credits came on the screen.

"Long." Quinn stretched and yawned. "Next time, remind me to lay in a supply of popcorn." He reached for the remote control and turned the windows back to normal. Late-afternoon sunshine streamed across the room.

He had obviously forgotten her request to see the Traveling Man tape, or else he didn't care to sit through it again himself just now and was hoping she would take the hint.

"Well, it did pass a couple of hours pleasantly enough. Not everything has to contain a larger message." She fumbled for her shoes and stood up, trying in vain to smooth some of the wrinkles out of her skirt. "If you've got other things to do, I can call a cab."

"Nothing important. I'll take you home."

The anticlimactic end to the afternoon made Emily feel rather sad, and then foolish. What had she expected? And even if he had kissed her again, she knew better than to think it was anything important.

In Brookside, he walked her to the door. Emily debated whether to invite him in, but before she'd made up her mind, he said goodbye. She must have looked surprised, for he added, "That's Brenna's Porsche in front of the house, and I'm not ready yet to be pinned down about performing in her wedding."

"I know, you're holding out for another cheesecake."

Quinn smiled. "Wouldn't you?" He brushed a kiss across her lips, a caress so light and quick she couldn't even react before it was over. "Tell her I'll call her tonight."

Brenna was standing on a low stool in the middle of the front parlor while Carrie, sitting on the floor, checked the length of her wedding gown.

Carrie took a couple of pins out of her mouth and looked up at Emily. "You must have gotten out of the station early."

"It's been a very strange day. Quinn brought me home."

Brenna sighed. "And then disappeared, of course. Isn't that just like the man? It's easier to get a grip on mercury than to pin him down."

Carrie was frowning. "What happened to your car?"

Emily blinked. "Darn, I left it at the station this morning and forgot it completely." She caught a glimpse of the expression on Brenna's face—a look of fascination, as if she would dearly love to know how and where Emily had spent the intervening hours—and stopped. "Never mind. I'll get out of your way so you can finish the fitting."

Carrie called her back just as she reached the hallway. "Brenna brought wedding invitations for both of us, Emily. Are you free on Saturday?"

"I realize it's terribly rude of me to leave it so late," Brenna admitted airily. "And yes, before you start wondering, I have ulterior motives for wanting you to come to my wedding."

She thinks if I'm there Quinn will happily take part, Emily thought. She was beginning to understand why Quinn was suspicious of his cousin's motives. Brenna was wrong, of course, but it was funny that they'd both come up with the same idea—inviting Emily—for such different reasons.

"In case I put my heel through my hem two minutes before the ceremony, I want Carrie to be on hand to patch me up," Brenna went on.

Carrie adjusted another pin. "You're not going to tear anything."

Brenna patted Carrie's shoulder comfortingly. "Of course I won't, not with you right there. But if you weren't, I'd be nervous and frantic, and anything might happen. So you see how important it is that you—"

"And why do you need me, Brenna?" Emily asked.

"To carry your grandmother's sewing basket, of course." The sparkle of mischief in Brenna's enormous eyes was unmistakable. "What did you think? That I wanted you as bait for Quinn? I'd never dream of doing such a thing."

Emily started to laugh. "Unless, of course, you thought it might work."

"Well, Emily—" Brenna's voice dropped to a conspiratorial whisper "—would it?"

Of course it wouldn't, Emily thought. Quinn had no serious interest in her....

EARLY MORNING was much more pleasant now that spring was moving on and each day was slightly longer. But it was still dark the next morning when Emily crept down the stairs, wrapped in a terry bathrobe, her hair wet from the shower.

She was greeted by the sound of water gurgling through the coffeepot. As she came in, Carrie lifted the lid of the waffle iron and tested the temperature before she poured batter onto the hot grids. She studied Emily's bathrobe and raised an eyebrow. "Aren't you feeling well?"

"I'm fine. I'm just calling a cab." She started flipping through the Yellow Pages.

"I can take you to work."

"It's no big deal. I should have picked the car up last night, but you were busy and I was lazy, so this morning I pay the price." She was just starting to dial when a knock sounded quietly on the back door. Carrie answered it.

"I came to chauffeur Emily to the station," Quinn announced. "We seem to have gotten too absorbed in other things yesterday to remember her car."

Carrie didn't even turn a hair. "That's very thoughtful of you, Quinn. Come and have breakfast while Emily gets dressed." She spun the golden-brown waffle onto a plate and set it on the kitchen table.

Quinn looked at it admiringly before cutting the crisp surface with a fork. "Don't mind if I do."

"That's my waffle you're eating," Emily complained.

"Does your grandmother always treat you like this in the mornings?" Without waiting for an answer, he turned to Carrie. "Do you have a room for rent?"

Emily gave up and went upstairs. When she came back, wearing tailored slacks and a cotton sweater, Quinn was just starting on his second waffle. She sat down across from him with her coffee.

Quinn looked her over. "That's much better than your usual morning garb. Tell me, did you dry your hair to impress me?"

"No. I figured you wouldn't be finished eating any time soon, and obviously I was right. By the way, if you make any comments on the show about how I look in a robe, I won't be responsible for what I do."

Quinn shrugged. "This isn't the first time I've seen you in a robe, but I haven't breathed a word about it yet. You can trust me. Eat, you'll feel better."

Emily sighed. "I can't help it. I had a nightmare about finding a pink slip tacked to my dressing-room door."

"And then what would Jason do?" Quinn scoffed. "Play organ music for two hours every morning till Gary recovers?"

"Believe it or not, Quinn, there are a number of people who would leap at the chance to fill in, because they think 'Kansas City Morning' is the pinnacle of success."

"And you agree with them?"

"I don't know what I think anymore. I only know life was a whole lot simpler a couple of weeks ago." She pushed her waffle aside, half-eaten. "Let's go."

But he was right; at the station everything appeared to be normal. There were no memos from Jason Manning and no messages from Gary, so she relaxed a little.

There were also no scouts in the audience, for Emily looked in vain as she worked her way down the aisle toward the set. But of course after the fiasco yesterday's show had been, that was no surprise. If Brad was right, and those three men were actually scouts, they probably hadn't stopped running till they hit Los Angeles.

She took her place beside Quinn. "I see Tish removed the table. I wonder if Brad's noticed yet."

"He's down in the newsroom, very subdued—except for a few snide remarks about us leaving together yesterday and coming in together this morning."

"Thanks. That's all I need to brighten my day."

"Of course, he also commented on the fact that your car was in the parking lot overnight. But obviously everything else is all right. You didn't get a pink slip, or you wouldn't be up here."

Emily sighed. "Apparently I've been worried about nothing," she admitted. "I was sure once Gary had cooled off about Brad he'd go after us, but apparently he didn't even notice all the give-and-take yesterday. At least, there wasn't a note waiting for me this morning. Did you get one?"

Quinn shook his head. "Not a word."

Brad did not appear, and the show started on a low-key note, much more modestly than any in the past week. Emily supposed the downturn was inevitable; there was no way to keep up forever the manic energy they had started with. Nevertheless, the change made her feel a little sad. She was almost going to miss that feeling of being constantly on edge, as if she were riding a hurricane. The ordinary stresses of live television seemed mundane in comparison.

Quinn reached into his pocket and pulled out an envelope.

Emily eyed it with distaste. "Please, I can't stand any more names for Robin's baby."

"Oh, thanks for reminding me of that. The contest entries are beginning to flood in already."

"Flood?"

"Well, I got two," Quinn admitted. "A teacher named Read and Wright, and a mapmaker named Turn Wright—"

"Or Bear Wright," Emily said.

"See? I knew you were enjoying this, no matter what you said. But guess what else was waiting for me this morning." He waved the envelope under her nose. "Two tickets to the Hunter Dix concert, courtesy of the promoter."

"Honestly?" Emily tried to snatch the envelope.

"Patience, dear. He heard me say on yesterday's show that you were brokenhearted, so—"

"He sent me tickets? Isn't that thoughtful! Let me see."

"Don't forget the envelope's addressed to me," Quinn reminded. "He sent *us* tickets."

Emily shrugged. "That's a mere detail. A gift to one of us—"

"Is a gift to both, of course. I'm glad to hear you admit it finally."

Emily wanted to hit herself in the head. Even when she was on guard, she couldn't seem to avoid giving him straight lines.

Quinn waited for the audience reaction to die down, then said gently, "And that reminds me. Don't you think it's time you gave in, Emily, and said those three special little words that every man in my position waits and hopes to hear?"

Every member of the studio audience gasped in unison. Emily's mind went totally blank for one long-drawn-out moment. Three special little words? *I love you,* of course.

This time Quinn had really gone too far. If he thought she was going to perjure herself for the sake of the ratings by declaring that she loved him, he was in for a surprise.

But it wouldn't be a lie, a quiet little voice whispered at the back of her mind. If she said those three special little words, she would be telling the absolute truth.

CHAPTER NINE

SHE HAD FALLEN IN LOVE with Quinn.

But one couldn't fall in love so quickly; the whole notion was preposterous. And even if the idea itself wasn't absurd, she absolutely, positively couldn't be in love with Quinn. She found him attractive, yes, there was no denying that, but she couldn't love a man who for days had been flirting with her just to stimulate the ratings. She was being ridiculous.

On the other hand, there was the way she practically went up in flames whenever he touched her. And if she was merely attracted to the man, why did she have to keep reminding herself that their whole relationship was just an act?

Quinn was still waiting, and looking at her inquiringly. "You know, darling," he prompted. " 'Here's the news.' "

The audience released its collective breath in a long, good-natured boo.

Quinn, feigning astonishment, looked out across the rows of seats. "Now what did you expect her to say?" he asked innocently.

Absolutely impossible, Emily told herself. The mere idea that she could fall in love with a man who was capable of *that* . . .

But wasn't that quicksilver unpredictability of his part of what had attracted her in the first place? Not only was he genuinely fun to be with, he provided a constant challenge to her own wits.

Emily leaned forward and gently patted his knee. "Anything you say," she murmured.

Quinn's eyes brightened. "Now that's not a bad phrase, either. As a matter of fact, I like your three words even better than mine."

"Somehow I thought you might." She looked directly into the camera. "Brad, what's in the news this morning?"

She got through the rest of the show, but she didn't remember much of what happened. She must have covered up her preoccupation well, however, for not even Quinn commented. At her dressing-room door after the show, he said, "What's your schedule like today?"

"I have a ribbon-cutting at eleven, followed by some serious reading and a tennis lesson. Why?"

"Oh, I forgot the ribbon-cutting."

"Forgot it?" Emily looked up at him in surprise. "Aren't you going?"

Quinn shook his head. "They didn't ask for me."

"Since when did that stop you?" Emily asked dryly.

He grinned and spread both hands flat on her door on either side of her. Though he wasn't touching her, she was effectively pinned between his arms. "Tell the truth, Em. You're going to miss me, aren't you?"

The breathless little ache in her chest was answer enough for Emily, but she could hardly admit it to him. She managed to say, "Like I miss a headache after it's gone."

His eyes began to sparkle, and his hands slid down the door and came to rest on her shoulders. "Really?"

Emily ducked her head. "Where are you going, anyway?"

"Is that a note of worry I hear in your voice? Don't fret. I'll be out on the road for the rest of the day, but I'll be here tomorrow. I wouldn't dream of walking out on you."

"Or the show," she said. She wasn't talking to him as much as reminding herself of what was really important.

"Of course." His lips brushed the sensitive triangle under her left ear. "See you tomorrow."

The words were commonplace, but his tone turned the phrase into an assignation—at least it might have done, if Emily hadn't been on her guard.

She sat patiently while Joanie restyled her hair for her public appearance and was surprised when the woman said, "You've been rubbing the side of your neck a lot this morning. Have you got an earache or something?"

Emily's fingertips dropped away from the triangle beneath her ear as if she'd been burned. "Of course not."

Heartache was more like it, she thought. She had been telling herself all morning that it was impossible to fall in love with someone in the space of a week. But Quinn wasn't an ordinary someone, and this hadn't been an ordinary week.

Emily had dated a man for more than a year once, and yet she hadn't known as much about him as she knew about Quinn in just these few short days.

Of course, in a way she had known Quinn much longer than that. Each day for the past three months, as she had watched his stories, she had observed his good-natured humor and his unique way of looking at the world—the very things she had, on close acquaintance, come to find so attractive.

All right, she asked herself, was what she was feeling actually only respect for his talent, admiration for a professional and perhaps—thrown in for good measure—a crush on a handsome celebrity?

But she honestly could find no hint of hero worship in her feelings. She might have if she wasn't involved in the field herself, but Emily knew the stresses of a life lived in the public eye. She realized how many people who lived that way succumbed to the temptation to think themselves greater than human.

No, if she was the kind to be fooled by a handsome face and a pretty manner on camera, she'd have been just as impressed with Brad Jarrett. But Quinn wasn't the sort of star who fell to pieces on closer acquaintance. He was real.

And so were her feelings for him. She might just as well admit it.

Deciding what she ought to do about those feelings was something else altogether.

THE CHURCH WAS almost full when Emily and Carrie reached the big doors that led into the sanctuary, and they waited for a couple of minutes before a young usher appeared. To Emily's relief it was not Quinn, though she knew he was taking part in the ceremony, after all. Brenna had mentioned the fact as she stood in the bride's dressing room and patiently allowed Carrie to tug each fold of her veil into place. And after she'd said it, she'd winked at Emily.

"Bride's side or groom's?" the usher asked, and solemnly offered an arm to each of them.

Emily tucked her hand into the curve of his elbow. "The bride's, please." At least she didn't have to stroll up the long aisle of this elegant church on Quinn's arm. It would be much easier to get through the ceremony if she didn't see him at all until it started, for then she would be less tempted to think of Quinn as the groom and herself as the bride....

Though of course, she told herself, weddings had no place at all in her dreams right now. For her, it would be more than enough to know that Quinn cared even a little about her, and that "Kansas City Morning" would go on as it was for a while. She and Quinn would have time to explore their feelings, and maybe someday...

But the image of herself in a full-skirted gown of drifting white lace and taffeta, walking up a long aisle toward an altar where Quinn waited, sprang into her mind so easily it was impossible to believe she'd never considered it before.

So much for her attempts to convince herself that all she really wanted was a little time to get to know him better and to give her feelings a chance to develop into something more.

She didn't realize Quinn was behind her until he spoke. "Aaron, if you don't mind, let me seat the loveliest lady in the church."

Emily turned her head with a jerk. He smiled angelically at her, then offered his arm to Carrie and started up the long aisle.

Emily obediently followed two steps behind, her hand still on Aaron's arm.

Quinn looked only slightly less wonderful in black evening clothes than he had at the celebrity auction in white tie and tails. He also appeared to be having a splendid time. At the moment, his head was bent slightly toward Carrie as if fascinated by what she was saying, and his free hand was cupped protectively over hers as it rested in the curve of his elbow. The tall candles lining the wide aisle cast a golden glow that made his sun-streaked hair look as if it had been sprinkled with stardust.

He led them almost to the front of the church. Emily heard him tell Carrie, "From here, you'll have the best possible view of that incredible dress." It was a far cry from the discreet back corner Emily would have chosen; she was glad she'd selected a wide-brimmed hat, for with a mere modest tip of her head she could hide her face.

At the reception, however, held at one of Kansas City's most exclusive clubs, there was no hiding at all. Before Emily could fade gracefully into a recess of the elegant ballroom, Brenna's mother hurried up and enthusiastically embraced Carrie.

"What a hit the dress was!" Grace Channing exclaimed. "Did you hear the gasp in the church when Brenna came down the aisle?" She smiled fondly at Emily. "I'm so glad you could come, dear. Lucky girl, I can't help but wonder what your grandmother plans to do with *your* wedding gown. It will be spectacular, I'm sure."

Emily gulped. The woman sounded as if she was waiting for an announcement, for heaven's sake!

Carrie smiled. "Of course it will," she murmured. "I've been thinking about it since she was born. Someday— whenever Emily decides she's ready—we'll get to work."

Bless you, Gran, Emily thought. Of course Brenna's mother hadn't been fishing for a specific date; if Emily hadn't been dreaming of weddings herself, she would never have suspected hidden meanings in the casual comment. "Someday," she agreed with a smile. "But I can't possibly look as stunning as Brenna did today."

Grace preened a bit. "She is a beautiful bride, isn't she? Oh, pardon me, I'm so flustered I've completely forgotten my manners." She turned to the woman who stood beside her. "Let me introduce my sister, Fiona Randolph."

Emily looked into dark eyes as large and brilliant as Quinn's were. But while Quinn's gaze was full of humor, Fiona Randolph's seemed to hint at pain endured and conquered, and Emily remembered what he had said about his mother's long illness.

"I hope Grace and her questions haven't embarrassed you," Fiona said. "She's been thinking about weddings for so long she's forgotten there's any other subject." Her voice was warm and her smile pleasant, and she held Emily's hand longer than a simple greeting required.

Grace laughed. "Don't mind Fiona. She's not lucky enough to have daughters, so she's just jealous." She patted Emily's shoulder and drifted off to greet other guests.

Fiona smiled. "That's a very old argument," she said. "I'm one of your devoted fans, you know, Emily."

"How sweet of you." Emily could feel a tiny pulse beat at the base of her throat. A long-standing fan, she wondered, or only one since Quinn had joined the show? And, no matter which it was, what did Quinn's mother think of the new "Kansas City Morning"?

Fiona seemed to read her mind. "I started watching a couple of years ago to fight off boredom while doing my morning exercise and therapy."

"Quinn mentioned that you'd been ill."

"Did he? When you joined the show, however, I suddenly found my morning routine much more inviting. You're my reward for good behavior, Emily."

Emily turned the comment over in her mind and smiled. "What a lovely compliment!"

"And recently, since Quinn's been there too..."

But Fiona didn't finish, for Quinn appeared with a tray of champagne glasses obviously filched from a passing waiter. "Isn't anyone taking care of you people?" he demanded, and presented the tray to Carrie first with a slight bow.

"Shouldn't you be dancing with the bridesmaids?" Emily asked as she picked up a glass. She didn't know whether to be annoyed at missing Fiona's opinion or glad he'd interrupted. Fiona, sipping champagne, didn't seem inclined to continue.

"I already have. And now that I'm finished with that, I'm free to enjoy myself." Quinn smiled contentedly. "I told Brenna I'd only come if she didn't make me sit at the head table like a good little robot." He took the last glass and set

the tray aside. "I may have started a new trend in weddings—where the bridal party can actually have fun."

"By pretending to be waiters?" Emily sipped her champagne. "Somehow I think you may be wrong about the
trend."

Quinn lifted the wide-brimmed white straw hat off her
head and set it on a nearby table. When Emily protested, he
said mildly, "I like to see who I'm arguing with. Besides,
you won't be very comfortable wearing that on the dance
floor."

"Who says we're going to dance?"

His eyes were alight with mischief. "*I* certainly didn't,"
he said gently.

Emily thought about it. He was correct; he hadn't issued
an invitation.

Quinn went on without mercy, "But I suppose I could
take pity on you, Emily." He removed the glass from her
hand and set it aside. "After all, it wouldn't look good for
you to be a wallflower now that you've been named as one-
half of Kansas City's most romantic couple." He guided her
toward the dance floor in the center of the room.

Emily was too startled to object. "You're kidding."

"Of course not. It'll be an item in one of the gossip col-
umns next week."

"Why? Because you planted it?"

"I might have, if I'd thought of it. I got a warning from
a confidential source at the newspaper who—"

A plump little matron, probably in her sixties, hurried
toward them. "Quinn, darling, mind your manners and introduce me to Emily." She stuck out her hand. "I'm
Quinn's mother's cousin Lucille, and I have been dying to
meet you!"

Quinn shrugged a little, as if to say he'd be happy to mind
his manners if Lucille would give him a chance.

Emily smiled impishly at him. Quinn might be asked for his autograph in public, but she was creating a stir in the heart of his family. It was a particularly sweet form of repayment for the way he'd teased her that day in the restaurant in Topeka.

Lucille hadn't stopped talking. "When is Gary coming back to 'Kansas City Morning'? Now that you've got the studio audience, I can hardly wait—I've wanted to meet him for years. Can you get me tickets to the first show when he gets back?"

Quinn gave a choked gurgle of a laugh.

Emily thought about giving him a swift kick in the ankle. She smiled at Lucille, instead. "Well, I don't know when that will be. He's at home now, but it may be a while before he's back to work. You could write to the station, and be sure to mention that you want to see Gary. It might not be the first show, but I'm sure they'll try to get you in right away."

Lucille accepted the advice and Emily's card, and went off to seek out a friend she'd spotted across the room. Quinn drew Emily into his arms as a slow and lazy love song started.

"Well, not everybody can adore us," she said.

"That's right. Some people have very bad taste." But the self-mocking note she had expected to hear was missing from his voice. "I didn't even know Gary was out of the hospital. You might have told me."

"I suppose I forgot about it." Emily didn't look at him. "He was released Thursday. I stopped at the hospital to see him that afternoon, but he'd already gone home."

"And it didn't occur to you that I'd like to know?"

"The show was so busy yesterday, and then you went out with the crew again afterward...." Her voice trailed off lamely.

The truth, she admitted, was that she hadn't forgotten about Gary at all. She simply hadn't wanted to tell Quinn, for doing so meant she had to face up to the inevitable end of their time together, and she didn't want to even think about that.

As long as she didn't admit that Gary would be returning soon, she could hold on to her dream—that he would retire early, leaving her and Quinn to carry on as a team. Then they would build the show into the masterpiece it could be. She and Quinn and "Kansas City Morning" would be the best of all possible worlds.

So far, so good. But it was the rest of the dream that really caused the problems, the part that had nothing to do with the show—the persistent little hope that whispered in the back of her mind that perhaps the two of them could be together forever.

The silence between them lengthened as the music lazily washed over the dancers. Emily wondered what Quinn was thinking, but she was afraid to ask.

EMILY CAME into the studio a few minutes early on Monday. Quinn was nowhere to be seen, but the audience seats were already almost full. A young woman in a front-row aisle seat waved an autograph book at her, and Emily paused to sign it. The woman glanced at the page, hugged it to her chest and said, "Oh, this is wonderful. I can't believe it, a front-row seat and now being able to talk to you! The only way to make it better would be if Quinn kissed you right on the show today."

Emily shook her head. "I'm afraid you're likely to be disappointed."

"Oh, I know he probably won't do it. He's got such self-control. But still, it's so romantic, the way he looks at you as if he's just dying to grab you and kiss you." Her voice dropped. "What's it like to kiss him?"

Emily blinked. "Now why would you suppose I know?" She gave the woman's shoulder a friendly squeeze and hurried on toward the stage. But her composure was shaken a little, not only by the question itself but by the memories it roused. She could almost smell the leather seats of the limousine, and the rose he wore, and the tang of his cologne...

Self-control. Yes, Quinn had plenty of that. She could use a little more herself. She swallowed hard, trying to push the image out of her mind before the tiny trickle of remembered excitement could build into a torrent. She had a show to do.

She settled into her tall chair and studied the note card that listed the morning's guests in order. She didn't look up, but she knew the instant Quinn came into the studio.

There was nothing magical about that, she told herself, for the audience had come to complete silence for a split second. She'd have had to be deaf not to notice.

"Good morning," he said as he took the chair beside her. "Didn't Joanie show up to take care of you today?"

"Of course. Why?"

"You look as if someone forgot to brush your hair, that's why. No. I've got it." His voice dropped. "Someone's been running his fingers through those lovely curls."

"The audience probably thinks it's you."

"Of course they do. Who *was* the lucky guy?"

It obviously didn't matter to him, did it? Emily handed him the cue card. "I'll give Joanie your compliments."

The corner of his mouth twitched.

Emily let her gaze sweep over the audience, noticing a familiar face here and there. She was surprised, with the demand for tickets, that there was room for repeat visitors. Or had the requests for seats already settled to a steadier pace? She supposed she shouldn't be surprised if the immediate rush was over. Even a hit Broadway show couldn't keep people standing in line at the ticket office forever.

The idea made her gloomy, but then she'd been feeling a little down since Saturday. Though Quinn had been nearby through most of the wedding reception, he hadn't monopolized her. And he hadn't offered to see her home, either.

Once Gary came back, she probably wouldn't see Quinn much at all.

Stop it, she told herself. That kind of thinking was only going to cause her more pain.

She studied the audience again as she clipped her microphone into place. There were half a dozen familiar faces; even the grandmotherly type who last week had been too busy crocheting even to shake Emily's hand was here again. Her bright-colored afghan had grown in the meantime, and it now covered the lower half of her body and trailed onto the floor.

Quinn said, "Don't forget the interview right after the show."

"The newspaper people?" Emily sighed. "Is this the same newspaper that's running the gossip about the most romantic couple?"

"How'd you guess?"

"I still don't think it's such a good idea to give this interview. Gary will be seething, and—"

"But Jason thinks it's wonderful that we're a phenomenon."

"A short-lived one, it looks like." She nodded toward the audience. "Haven't you noticed our repeat customers? Ticket requests must be down."

Quinn shook his head. "Hardly. Some of them were standing in line this morning without tickets. Tish finally gave up and let them fill in the no-shows' seats."

"Well, that's a comfort. I was beginning to think our fan club was dying before it even got off the ground."

Tish's signal from the control room caught Emily's eye, and she glanced at the monitor just as the main camera went live. Another show to get through.

No, it was another show to enjoy. And she was going to treasure every moment of it—for she didn't know how many more there might be.

THEY TOOK OVER Jason Manning's office for the interview at his invitation. "The dressing rooms around here are notoriously small," he told the reporter with a smile. "We can't have you seeing those and telling the world, can we? Leave people their image of big spaces with whirlpool tubs and chaise lounges."

Emily curled up on the end of Jason's couch in an almost defensive posture. Quinn sat down beside her, leaving a very proper foot of space between them. Emily thought she saw the reporter lift an eyebrow at that.

However, to Emily's relief, the woman didn't even mention the most-romantic-couple nonsense. Instead, she asked deep thoughtful questions about them and about the show, and eventually Emily began to relax. Though the questions weren't easy, they were intriguing, and Emily even found herself talking about the days of her childhood, when Carrie had been deeply involved in the theater.

"After my parents divorced, my mother and I lived with Gran," she said. "She was often handed tickets along with her pay, so I not only met the celebrities when they came for fittings, but I saw them onstage, as well. That wonderful contrast between the real person and the character fascinated me, and I suppose that's part of why I do this now.''

The reporter smiled encouragingly.

"I enjoy learning about our guests," Emily went on. "What they're like in private life, as well as what their public interests are. And I love having time for more than just a few sentences about a new book, or a couple of minutes of film clips. That's the best thing about the new format. I'd expand it even more if I could.''

"And you, Quinn?" The reporter turned to him. "Do you miss tramping all over the world covering important events?"

She said it as if she knew where he'd been, Emily thought. That was odd; Quinn had said once that he'd worked here and there, but...

"You won a Peabody prize a few years ago for investigative reporting," the reporter went on. "Now you're interviewing movie stars.''

Quinn shrugged. "I see my job as making the world better. There are lots of ways to do that.''

Emily hardly heard his answer. *A Peabody?* The words struck her like a hammer. The Peabody was the ultimate prize in broadcast reporting, the equivalent of the Pulitzer—the dream of every television reporter.

She rummaged through her memory, but she couldn't recall anything about Quinn's winning a Peabody. Of course, there were a fair number of these prizes, awarded in numerous categories, and she would have had no reason a few years ago to notice Quinn Randolph's name above any of the others.

But that didn't lessen the shock. Why hadn't he told her about it? When she had asked him what he used to do, why had he passed it off so casually, as if it didn't matter?

The reporter's voice was full of doubt. "But don't you regret the critical stories you're missing—the droughts and famines, the destruction of rain forests, the earthquakes, the political upheavals?"

Emily heard Quinn say something about deep stories being seen by a few people and never heard of anymore. She wasn't really listening. The blood was pounding in her ears. She tried to reason herself out of her fury; why should she be so upset, anyway?

Because it was important, and he hadn't thought enough of her to mention it. He hadn't cared enough to want to share that critical part of his life, his history....

"And in the future?" the reporter asked. "Will you be staying with 'Kansas City Morning' or moving back to something more news oriented—in New York, perhaps?"

Quinn smiled. "I've been talking to people about some projects, but for now I'm just waiting to see what the best offer is. I'm sure you understand why I can't go into detail."

What a fool I've been, Emily thought. She had let herself hope that if Gary didn't come back, Quinn would contentedly settle into the host's chair on "Kansas City Morning" and stay there forever. It had seemed so logical, and so perfect.

What she hadn't realized until just now was that she had planned much further than that. She had simply postponed her dream, not given it up. She had convinced herself that even if Gary did come back, he wouldn't be staying forever; with his health to consider, he might not fill out his contract. And even if he did, three years wasn't such an awfully long time to wait. Quinn could fill in for Gary on vacations in the meantime....

What a beautiful little world she had created!

Of course, Quinn had never said he would be interested in anything of the sort. Emily had jumped to conclusions because she knew he was tired of being on the road—and because she wanted so much for him to feel as she did. But just because she thought "Kansas City Morning" was the pinnacle of her dreams—if only she could share it with Quinn—didn't mean Quinn felt the same way.

He didn't want the show, or he wouldn't be negotiating for something else. And even more obviously, he didn't want Emily. If he had, he'd have shared his past with her—and his hopes for the future.

Quinn checked his watch. "I'm sorry, but I have a crew waiting for me. If you've finished . . ."

"Oh, of course." The reporter shut off her tape recorder and stood up. "The problem is I could sit and talk to you two all day." She shook hands with Emily and smiled at Quinn. "I'd like to hear all your war stories sometime."

They walked her to the station door, and Emily watched until the reporter was safely out of sight in the parking lot. Then she said, "I need to talk to you, Quinn."

He obviously caught the tense edge in her voice, for his eyebrows rose. "My dressing room or yours? Or shall we grab Jason's office again before he takes it back?"

Without quite knowing why, Emily led the way to Studio B, instead.

The set was dim, and the control booth was dark and empty. The only light came from exit signs and small safety bulbs here and there. The huge empty room should have seemed like an echoing warehouse, but the acoustics were so perfect that on the stage it was like talking across a coffee table.

Emily stood, her hands braced on the back of her tall chair. "You never told me about your prize."

"Well, it's not something I drop into first conversations." Quinn sounded a bit wary. "What would you have liked me to say? 'Hi, my name's Quinn and I won a Peabody once upon a time'?"

"That's the lamest excuse I've ever heard."

He frowned a little, but his voice was genial. "All right. How's this? The prize isn't all that important to me, and so I didn't even think about telling you. What's the big deal, anyway?"

"You don't know?"

"No, dammit, I don't know." Quinn pulled his chair around and sat down. "What are you talking about?"

Emily flung out her arms in a gesture which encompassed the entire studio. "This, the show, is important to me. You let me believe it was important to you, too!"

Maybe the accusation wasn't fair, she realized. She'd convinced herself without evidence. And yet, if "Kansas City Morning" didn't matter to him, why hadn't he left it as it was? He'd purposely set out to shake the show from its foundations. "You made a joke of it!"

"Now wait a minute, Emily."

"All you have to do is wave your Peabody prize, and any station in the country, even any network, would be eager to have you."

"I wouldn't be so sure about that." He slid out of his chair and came toward her.

"You didn't need to use 'Kansas City Morning' as a stepping stone to get what you want!"

His hands came to rest on her shoulders, almost tentatively. "What makes you so sure you know what I want?"

"Do the details matter? Whatever it is, you certainly aren't looking for it around here! I should have realized what was going on when you first called the show 'morning fluff.' What you've been doing for the last few years doesn't leave you much room to talk, but compared to earth-shattering news, of course 'Kansas City Morning' looks pretty unimpressive. I ought to have known from the beginning you were only amusing yourself.'' She caught herself up short. ''With the show, I mean. Don't flatter yourself that I took you seriously, because I didn't.''

''I'd like to know what you *were* thinking.'' His hands slipped off her shoulders, and he took half a dozen steps away from her, then back again. ''If, that is, you were thinking at all. What in hell do I have to do to get you to admit—''

''It was a great act, Quinn. But I'm glad it's almost over, because it's getting to be a strain to keep up the image. It will be such a relief in a few weeks when Gary's back, and I don't have to play a part anymore.''

The stage lights were so powerful they actually popped as they burst into life. Emily jumped, then spun to face the doorway.

Standing just inside the studio, taking notes on a clipboard, was Tish Grant. Behind her, his hand still on the row of light switches, was Gary Bennington.

''Those silly tall chairs have to go,'' Gary said. Then he saw the two on stage and paused.

''What perfect timing, Emily,'' Quinn murmured. ''Lucky you. The strain and stress are all over, and you don't even have to wait a few weeks. You've got your wish.''

He didn't even look at her as he spoke.

CHAPTER TEN

GARY MOVED BRISKLY toward the stage, rubbing his hands together. "Quinn, thanks for filling in." The note of dismissal in his voice was obvious. "There you are, Emily. Good. We need to have a chat right away."

"Welcome back, Gary. I'm so glad..." That you've recovered, she meant to say; nothing more. But Quinn was standing so close to her she could feel the sudden tightening of his body. She took an involuntary step toward the edge of the stage, away from him.

He apparently believed she would be happy if she never had to see him again. Well, why shouldn't he? She'd as much as told him so herself just a couple of minutes ago. And even though she hadn't meant it, she could hardly stand here now and explain. She might be a fool, but she wasn't idiot enough to confide that she was so desperately in love with him she couldn't bear the notion that for Quinn she'd been only a flirtation.

"Tish, the chairs go," Gary said. "Immediately. Did you get that? And move the love seat back to the middle of the stage."

Quinn hadn't moved. "Tell me, Gary, are you going to take a good look at the changes, or just reverse them automatically?"

Gary's eyes narrowed. "I'll take over from here, Quinn. Thank you very much."

The insincerity that dripped from his voice startled Emily. Gary had never pretended to like Quinn, but she hadn't anticipated this cold rejection of his professional opinions. After all, Gary hadn't argued about the changes earlier.

Was that only because he was more worried about Brad then? Or did he perhaps know that arguing with Quinn wouldn't get him anywhere, so he'd simply been biding his time?

She moved to the edge of the stage. "I like the chairs, Gary."

Even though he was standing well below Emily on the main floor of the studio, Gary gave the impression he was looking down his nose at her. "Of course, you didn't see the extent of leg you displayed while sitting in one of them. Speaking of which, some of your clothes in the last few shows have been outlandish. What in heaven's name happened to the wardrobe people, Tish?"

"She started to wear her own things," the director said. "And frankly, Gary, with the whole show falling to pieces under my feet, I didn't have time to fight about it."

What had Quinn said about the director that day over brunch in his town house? *Tish would cut your throat in a minute to save her job,* that was it. And though Emily had known he was probably right, she hadn't quite believed it in her heart until this moment.

She didn't realize how stunned she must have looked till Quinn moved to the edge of the stage beside her. She thought for a moment he was going to put a comforting hand on her shoulder, but instead, he folded his arms across his chest. "I encouraged her to dress differently, Gary," he said. "And I'm the one who changed the schedule and opened up the studio to the public and bought the chairs. Ask Tish. She'll tell you it wasn't Emily."

"Thanks," Emily managed. "I—"

Quinn didn't pause. "Emily did her level best to preserve the status quo for you, Gary. I, on the other hand, was simply trying to bring this show into the nineties." He looked down into Emily's eyes. "Good luck," he said huskily. "See you around—maybe."

Then he was gone before she could say more than his name. She had no chance to explain that her shock hadn't been a reaction to Tish's betrayal or even to Gary's coldness—but to the sudden realization that she might never again be truly comfortable on "Kansas City Morning." She started after him. She had to tell him—

Gary called her back. "Emily, we aren't finished." He sat down in the club chair, which had always been his favorite. "It's going to take a while to get the show back in shape, of course. I think the best way to handle this is for us to bring it out in the open tomorrow and discuss it on the air."

She paused at the edge of the set like a bird who was about to fly. "Discuss what, exactly?"

"The crazy events of the last couple of weeks, what else? Everybody who watches the show knows what a nut Quinn can be, just from seeing the Traveling Man segments. We'll just laugh it off, that's all."

"Turn it into a joke and go back to business as usual." Emily's tone was level.

"Of course. The sooner the audience realizes the last couple of weeks were only an unfortunate aberration, the sooner the damage can be repaired." He raised his voice. "Tish, be sure the announcer makes it clear during the show tomorrow that there will be no more live audiences, so that anybody who's still holding tickets won't turn up expecting a seat."

Emily murmured, "Wouldn't you enjoy doing that yourself, instead of letting the announcer have all the fun?"

Gary ignored her. "As for tomorrow, I suppose we'll have to post guards at all the station entrances to keep people out."

Tish looked doubtful. "Gary, they'll be very upset at being shut out. They already have tickets, and they've had no warning. Don't you think for just one day—"

The studio door opened again, and Jason Manning strode in. "Glad to see you, Gary," he said jovially. "They told me you were here checking to make sure we managed to hold things together while you were gone."

"Barely," Gary said crisply.

"I got the impression your doctors wanted you to rest for a couple of weeks more, Gary."

"By then I'd have had no show left. Is that what you had in mind, Jason?"

Emily held her breath.

But Gary didn't wait for an answer; he turned back to the director. "All right, Tish. I suppose we'll have to let ticket holders in tomorrow, but absolutely none after that."

Jason said plaintively, "The studio audience has been very well received."

"It's still my show, Jason, and I don't work with a studio audience. It's in my contract."

"I realize that. I just—"

Emily took a step forward. "You're making a big mistake, Gary. Jason's right. The studio audience is essential to the atmosphere of 'Kansas City Morning.' You can't get rid of it now, or you'll destroy the show."

The murderous look Gary gave her confirmed her earlier feelings. If she stayed, the atmosphere around Studio B wouldn't be just unpleasant from now on; it would be actively toxic.

"I'm afraid you have an inflated opinion of your judgment, Emily," he said smoothly.

She raised her eyebrows just a little. "And of my value, perhaps?"

"You've always overestimated that, I'm afraid."

Tish gave a tiny, almost imperceptible nod. Jason Manning moved closer to the stage, one hand raised in protest and his mouth open as if he wanted to intervene. Then he paused.

The battle lines were drawn, but Emily knew the outcome of the war was not in any doubt.

She could hang on for a while, but she would inevitably lose. With Gary and Tish cooperating, it would be only a matter of time till she was pushed out. There were all kinds of mild, almost unnoticeable—but dirty—tricks they could pull. It would be easy to leave her out of important interviews, to cut her airtime to a minimum, to make sure she ended up looking like nothing more than a decorative prop.

Jason Manning understood that, too, and it was obvious from his silence that he knew he couldn't stop that kind of quiet, behind-the-scenes sabotage. Nobody could, because Gary's contract gave him a kind of unbeatable power.

Even if Jason wanted her to stay on the show, even if he still intended to turn it over to her eventually, she couldn't stick it out for three long years while she waited for Gary to retire. Not under those conditions. If she tried, she would have no credibility left, no audience, no following. It would be worse than starting from scratch. And it was obvious to her now that Gary wouldn't be leaving a day earlier than he had to.

She turned on her heel and started for the door.

Gary's voice rang out. "Where are you going? Our discussion isn't finished."

"Yes, it is. I'm leaving. Quinn said I tried to keep things under control for you, but he wasn't telling the truth, Gary. I was very much involved in the changes, and I think they were necessary and wise. He was right—this show does need to come into the nineties.''

She brushed past Jason and he caught her arm. "Wait," he said under his breath. "Let's talk about this."

Emily shook her head. "I can see the handwriting on the wall, Jason. I don't think there's anything left to talk about."

"There isn't," Gary said. "Don't worry about giving your two weeks' notice—you're finished as of now. If we can get down to business, Jason . . ."

Emily put a hand on the producer's sleeve. "Jason, thank you for giving me this opportunity. I'll always appreciate your taking a chance on me."

He glanced at Gary. "Don't disappear, Emily. I want to talk to you."

"You know where to find me. But right now . . ."

He nodded. "I'll be in touch." He moved toward the set. "All right, Gary. Now that you've managed to get rid of the best chance this show had, what do you plan to do next?"

Emily was almost to the front door of the station before she realized that her handbag and car keys were still in her dressing room. Before she turned back to get them, she looked out across the parking lot. There was the usual bustle, but no big recreational vehicle parked just outside the door.

What did you expect? she chided herself. Had she seriously supposed that Quinn would read her mind and wait for her? And then they'd ride off together into the sunset?

What a fool she was to dream that there could still be a future for them!

It might be days before Quinn even showed his face in the station again now that he was free of the demands of "Kansas City Morning." And no matter when he came back, Emily wouldn't be there.

Jason Manning's secretary beckoned from her glass-enclosed office. Emily thought about pretending she hadn't seen the summons. It would be something about tomorrow's show, no doubt, and Emily didn't want to have to explain to the secretary that it no longer mattered. She didn't want to wait around for Jason, either. What could he have on his mind, anyway?

Another show? Perhaps, if he really didn't want to lose her. No, that wasn't likely; he could hardly have dreamed up any worthwhile project in the past five minutes. In any case, whatever it was, she'd much rather hear it tomorrow, when she wasn't quite so emotional.

But she'd better tell the secretary to call the newspaper and make sure this morning's interview didn't get into print and embarrass them all.

The secretary said, "Mrs. Temple would like to talk to you."

Till then, Emily hadn't noticed the woman sitting with her back to the glass wall, a bright-colored afghan cascading across her lap. Emily had seen that afghan before—on a couple of occasions, in fact—in the studio audience. She sighed. The last thing she needed right now was a devoted fan asking for an autograph.

It was odd, though, that a woman who hadn't spared time for a handshake from the star of the show on her first visit to the studio would go out of her way to meet her now. In spite of herself, Emily was intrigued.

Mrs. Temple's crochet hook didn't pause. "I'd like a few minutes, young lady." The words were firm, but the tone of voice was friendly.

"I'm sorry, I really don't have time..." Not true, Emily reminded herself. She had all the time in the world, since there was no show to prepare for tomorrow. And it wasn't Mrs. Temple's fault that Emily's day was turning out to be the worst in her life. "If you want an autograph," she said dryly, "I should warn you that it's particularly valuable, since it might be the last one I'm ever asked to sign."

Mrs. Temple looked at the secretary. "If you'll excuse us..."

To Emily's utter astonishment, the secretary meekly picked up a legal pad and a stack of mail and went out.

"Jason hasn't talked to you?" The crochet hook flashed in a hypnotic rhythm.

"I don't see why you think he should have. Who *are* you, anyway?"

"My name's Eleanor Temple, but I don't suppose that will mean much to you."

"Temple," Emily mused. "There's Temple Productions, but—"

A gleam of respect appeared in the woman's eyes. "Jason was right. You're very quick." She put the crochet hook down and folded her hands atop the bright yarn. "Yes, I'm a large part of Temple Productions. We're an independent company that produces shows for television syndication."

Brad was wrong, Emily thought. There hadn't been network scouts in the studio that day—just one small independent grandmotherly woman with an afghan.

"I have a business proposition for you, Emily. I want to put together a new morning show and offer it for syndication nationwide."

Emily's knees suddenly felt as insubstantial as tapioca pudding. She sat down more suddenly and less gracefully than ever before.

"I wanted to feature you and Quinn together, of course," Mrs. Temple said. "The atmosphere of controlled chaos that the two of you have created on the set is not only charming and intriguing, it's a completely new twist in morning television."

For one brief instant Emily could see it all—the show she had always wanted to do, a more brilliant jewel than "Kansas City Morning" could ever be, with a national audience, world-famous guests—and Quinn. Most important of all, Quinn.

Then she realized that Mrs. Temple had used the past tense.

The woman went on, "And even though Quinn isn't interested..."

Emily thought she had faced the death of all her dreams when Quinn had left the studio and the station this morning. But somewhere deep inside her, despite everything, one last tiny hope must still have lurked, for Mrs. Temple's words struck her like a blow. "Of course not," she said bitterly. "He wants bigger things."

Mrs. Temple's eyes were bright with interest, but she said only, "He's very talented. And so are you. Jason's right, you're far too good to stay local."

"Jason said that?" Emily's voice was faint. Someday, she knew, when she managed to get her balance back, she would treasure that compliment. At the moment, it was only a random bunch of words.

"And when I saw you in action, I agreed. We'll need to choose your cohost very carefully, of course, but I think that if we can reestablish that sparkle, we can take the competition by storm."

The show she had always wanted, the national audience, the world-famous guests—without Quinn?

Emily shook her head wordlessly. She knew it was rude and foolish and stupid to turn down such an offer without even offering a reason. But right now she hurt too much to try to explain.

Eleanor Temple folded the afghan and fitted it into the enormous knitting bag at her feet. From the side pocket of the bag she took an elegant, engraved business card and handed it to Emily. "You think it over. Let me know." She rose. "Just remember, Emily, this is the chance of a lifetime."

EMILY FELT NO BITTERNESS, just a deep and aching grief for the way things might have been. Eleanor Temple was right; she was offering the chance of a lifetime. But for Emily it was nothing without Quinn. No other partnership could produce the kind of magic that had sparked between the two of them, because she could never feel the same about any other man. Not professionally, and not personally.

And yet, even if Quinn hadn't turned down the opportunity, she would have found it impossible to work with him any longer. Their lighthearted appreciation of each other had vanished. She had killed what remained of it this morning, and without that, the sparkle had gone, as well. No, she had made the only choice she could.

She went home, hoping Gran would be too busy this morning to ask questions. If so, she could slip away by herself for a while, until she could sort out her confused feelings and know which ones she needed to talk about, and which ones she must keep inside her own heart forever.

The moment her car pulled into the driveway, Emily knew that Carrie Lambert was very busy indeed. Or rather, she soon would be.

But there was little relief for Emily in the knowledge. For parked beside the house was a large recreational vehicle, with the station logo and call letters on the side. On the lawn nearby stood Ivan and Murray, too absorbed in setting up equipment and checking supplies even to notice her presence. And somewhere inside the RV, no doubt—unless he was already with Carrie in the house—was the Traveling Man.

Brenna had brought him to Brookside in the first place because she thought he should do a story about Carrie Lambert. But he hadn't said a word about it since, and Emily had forgotten.

It was too late to retreat, so she got out of the car. As she said hello to Ivan and Murray, Quinn appeared in the RV's doorway. He was knotting his tie, and his hands stilled for an instant on the striped silk when he saw her.

"Quite a coincidence," Emily said. She bit her tongue as soon as the words were out; sounding catty was no way to start.

"As a matter of fact, that's exactly what it is. Why are you home at this hour?"

She might as well tell him; the news wasn't going to stay secret for long. "I'm getting a good start at being unemployed."

"Emily!" He leapt down from the step. "I'm sorry. I tried—"

"I know you did. Thank you for that." She tried to clear her throat, but it didn't help much; her voice was still husky. "At least I didn't get fired. I quit."

He looked at her in silence for so long that Emily began to fidget, biting on her thumbnail and shifting from one foot to the other. Then he looked at Ivan and Murray. "Pack all this up and go back to the station. Oh, and tell Mrs. Lambert I'll call her later to reschedule the shoot." He took the car keys out of Emily's hand. "Let's go somewhere quiet."

She didn't pay any attention to the direction he chose until he stopped the car at the edge of a park. He had chosen the least-used portion of it, and except for the occasional jogger and the muted noise of traffic from the nearby avenue, they could have imagined themselves entirely alone. The warm breeze was soft against Emily's face as they walked along a narrow path, and the aroma of spring flowers tugged at her senses.

Neither of them had spoken since they left the house, and the silence was wearing on Emily's nerves. She stopped beside a historical marker, one of a series explaining the progress of a Civil War battle that had taken place on the site. "I'm sorry," she said without looking at him. "I really overreacted this morning. Your career and your past are your own business, and there's no reason you should have told me about winning a Peabody."

Quinn's voice was quiet. "If I'd thought it was important, I would have."

She nodded. "I know." What he was really confirming, of course, was that he hadn't told her because *she* didn't matter. But it no longer hurt as much to admit that. Or perhaps she was just so numb that nothing could hurt much anymore.

"What are you going to do now?" Quinn asked.

"I don't know. Go back to radio maybe." She put her hands in the pockets of her skirt and walked on, slowly, with her head bent.

Quinn fell into step beside her. "There's a woman you should talk to."

"Eleanor Temple?"

"She caught you?"

"She made her pitch. Controlled chaos, a whole new style of morning television." It was too difficult to look into his eyes; she let her gaze fall to the asphalt path. "I said no."

"Why?" His voice was choked, as if he couldn't believe his ears.

Emily shrugged. "You said once I'm too naive and tenderhearted to survive in television, that I'd be eaten alive. I guess you're right."

"In many cases, yes—you're too trusting for your own good." Quinn stopped in the middle of the path and put his hands on her shoulders. "But you have a chance to start from scratch, Emily. You could put together the kind of crew you were talking about—a real team, where the show is the most important thing. How can you turn that down?"

She couldn't tell him that he was a big part of that dream, and without him none of it mattered. She shook her head. "Because I'm a fool, I guess. You shouldn't be surprised at that." She turned away to walk on and tried to force lightness into her voice. "She's awfully interested in you, Quinn. I'm sure if you approach the subject right, she'll work with you on the kind of show you want."

Quinn hadn't moved. "Once and for all, Emily, what do you think I want?"

She stopped a couple of paces away and looked up at him, confused by the hard note in his voice. "I don't know," she said tentatively. "But I'd like to."

Quinn gave a harsh laugh. "Well, I guess you're not the only fool in the world, and I might as well admit it. I want that new and improved morning show of Eleanor's—every bit as much as I suspect you want it."

Emily gulped, and the asphalt path seemed to rock beneath her feet. What was he trying to accomplish? Was it only a lovely lie, an effort to talk her into taking the chance he was so sure she ought to have? Or did he really mean it—that he honestly did want the show, so much that he'd even put up with her? But if that was the case, surely he wouldn't have turned Eleanor Temple down flat.

She laughed a little. "Oh, come on, Quinn. You can't be serious. You said yourself that morning TV's nothing but fluff. It's entertainment, and that's all it's supposed to be. So I'm afraid I don't understand why all of a sudden—"

"Of course you don't. You haven't been there." He propped one foot on a park bench and folded his arms on his knee. "Five years of chasing big stories around the world," he said almost to himself, "and what difference does it make? You do the story and you move on to the next one, and only the faces are different. Nobody remembers, and nothing changes. The same famines are going on in the same places, and after a while you start to believe they always will."

The pain in his voice could not be denied. "Oh, Quinn," she said helplessly.

"I saw too many people caught in the midst of forces they couldn't control—wars, famines, disease, earthquakes. When you watch enough of that, you start to get hard and cynical."

"But you aren't—"

"Not anymore perhaps. I came home because my mother was very ill, and for a year I did almost nothing. I was burned-out, Emily. Then the Traveling Man came along, and believe me, after five years of bad news, the chance to look at good news was very appealing. But now I'm ready for something deeper again."

"Deeper? A morning show? Quinn—"

"I have dreams and ideas for that show, just as you do. Visions of what it could be—a mix of entertainment and important issues. It can reach an audience that otherwise wouldn't be touched at all, an audience that doesn't give a damn about Peabody prizes. Those people are very much like I was when I came home, you see. It's not that they don't care, but when you don't feel you can do anything, it's easier to ignore the problem altogether. But when they understand that they do have power..." His reasoning, his passion, were almost hypnotic. "You gave me the idea yourself, you know."

"*I* did?" Emily could hardly believe her ears.

"That first day in the commissary, when you started spouting off about ethical standards and what 'Kansas City Morning' could be."

"I didn't have anything like this in mind," she admitted.

"Perhaps not, but you made me curious, and when I started thinking about the possibilities... At first, I didn't want anything to do with 'Kansas City Morning.'"

"I'd never have guessed," Emily said dryly.

"But with the very first show, I began to see the potential of the format itself. And then I realized what a magnificent team we made. You'd always been passive before, with Gary in charge. It used to make me mad to watch the show, because I thought there must be more to you than that. When I found out how much more there was—" he shook his head as if reliving the moment "—I knew then we could make a difference."

So he'd had his dreams, too. Emily had never considered anything on the scale of this brainstorm of his. "Why didn't you say something?"

Quinn shrugged. "It was just too crazy to talk about. We'd have to have the right sort of producer—one willing to take some risks—and the chance to draw a national audience. That combination didn't look very likely until Jason put me in touch with Eleanor yesterday."

Emily shook her head in confusion. "And she's willing to take the chance? Then why did you turn her down, Quinn?"

For a moment she thought he wasn't going to answer. Then he said, "Because it wouldn't work, Emily. The act could only go on so long, and I think we've worn it out."

She nodded sadly. "I know."

"And unless there was something more, something besides the act, then the banter would turn to bitterness. There wouldn't be any humor left. Just sour and hateful jabs at each other.''

Emily held on to the back of the park bench. The earth under her feet seemed to have suddenly turned into an old-fashioned carousel, and she was having trouble keeping her balance. Something more? Did he, could he, mean what she hoped he did?

"And if we can't share that opportunity," Quinn said softly, "then I want you to have your chance."

"Something besides the act?" she managed to say. "I don't know what you're talking about."

He set one foot on the bench and folded his arms on his knee. "You never have understood the chemistry between us, have you?"

Almost involuntarily, she shook her head.

"Or maybe I'm the one who didn't understand—because I honestly thought it was special."

But it was, Emily thought breathlessly. *It is!*

"We had a kind of magic together, Emily. I knew it almost from the first moment we were on the air, when the sparks started flying and the whole studio came alive. I thought you recognized it, too. I didn't understand till that day we went out on the road, and you wanted to put the brakes on the whole relationship, that maybe you didn't see it the same way. Maybe you weren't feeling the same thing I was."

Emily gulped.

"I set out to prove to you that what we had was unique, but the night of the celebrity auction I realized it was even more than that. That's when I knew I was in love with you. But you... didn't care."

And that was when she had made up her mind to keep things light at all costs, to never allow herself to think that this might be serious. In her fear that he couldn't possibly

care about her, that it was only a game to him, she had
squashed the very thing she wanted most. Unable to speak,
she put out a hand to him, but he didn't see.

"You were just playing along because I hadn't left you a
choice," Quinn went on. "Just marking time till things got
back to normal. And still, I couldn't help falling a little
harder every time I saw you." He straightened up, with the
air of a man lifting a burden he expected to carry for a long
time.

"We could still do the show." She hardly recognized her
own voice. "Together."

Quinn shook his head. "Didn't you hear me, Emily? I
can't work with you like that again. I need too much more."
He started to stride away, then turned and tossed her car
keys to her. "Don't worry about me. I'm going to take a
long walk."

Don't just stand here, Emily told herself frantically. But
her feet seemed to be frozen to the path. "You asked why I
turned down Eleanor's offer," she called after him. "And
I didn't really answer you."

He stopped, but he didn't turn around.

"You said you were looking for other projects," she said,
"waiting for the best deal. I didn't even think about what
kind of thing you wanted. I just knew it didn't seem to leave
any room for me."

Slowly he turned to face her. His eyes were full of uncertainty. "It mattered?"

Emily nodded. "And Eleanor hadn't even finished telling me about the show yet when she said you weren't interested, so..."

"I told her that this morning, after our little...spat."

That made sense; considering the things she'd said to him
in the studio, he certainly wouldn't have nourished hopes of
working together on anything. "I didn't know when you'd

said it, but I thought you meant you didn't want to work with me at all."

"No. Oh, Emily, we could be great partners, if only..."

She smiled at him and saw the uncertainty in his eyes give way to wonder. "I knew I couldn't do a show with someone else once I'd known that magic you were talking about—with you. There would always be something missing." She tried to steady her voice. "Something far more important than just being cohosts."

He held out his arms, and she ran straight into them. A delicious little shiver shook her body as she pressed against his comforting warmth.

"I need you so badly, Quinn," she whispered. "And I was so afraid I was a fool to let myself love you, when all you wanted to do was tease me."

There was nothing teasing about the way he kissed her, as if he never intended to let go of her again. And later, when he stopped kissing her and held her a couple of inches away from him, he looked down into her eyes and said, "We'd better get married before the new show starts."

Emily was feeling too dizzy to argue. "Anything you say. But why?"

"Because right now we can get by with a small crowd. If we wait, we'll have to invite the whole country."

"Oh." She shook her head a little to clear the haze. "You might be right. Assuming, of course, we're a hit."

"We will be. Together, we can't fail." He kissed her again and after a while said thoughtfully, "How about getting away from it all on a honeymoon?"

"How far away?" Emily asked doubtfully.

"We could go river rafting. I've always wanted to drift down the Mississippi like Huck Finn."

Something about that didn't sound quite right, but Emily couldn't put her finger on the problem. She looked up at him warily.

"Just you and me and Ivan and Murray," Quinn said happily. "We could start in St. Louis and go all the way to New Orleans."

"Ivan and Murray?"

"Well, I can't just lay them off without notice."

"Don't you want them to work on the new show?"

"Of course, but they have to do something in the meantime. Rafting down the Mississippi would make a great series to finish out the Traveling Man. Besides, think of the publicity we'd—"

Emily stood on her toes and silenced him with a kiss, long and slow and sensual.

When she was finished, Quinn cleared his throat and said slowly, "On the other hand, maybe we'll just leave Ivan and Murray at home."

"Whatever you say," she murmured. "You always come up with the best ideas, my love."

EPILOGUE

NOT A SINGLE EMPTY SEAT could be found in the studio that
day. There was usually a waiting list for tickets, but the demand had been particularly heavy for this show, their second anniversary on the air.

Emily took her eye off the monitor for a moment and
looked out at the audience. They seemed to be enjoying the
videotape recap of the show's first two years. Emily had had
her doubts, but Ivan and Murray had been so excited by the
idea that she hadn't had the heart to use her veto power. Of
course, she hadn't expected them to go quite so far afield—
there was no excuse for that clip of Emily in her wedding
gown feeding Quinn a slice of cake; that had been a full
month before the show had even gone on the air.

But the fast-changing collage of guests and the half-
minute film of the night they'd been presented a national
award for public service were wonderful memories.

When the tape ended, she had to blink a bit, not only because the studio lights had suddenly come on again but to
hold back happy tears. She glanced at Quinn and saw the
sympathetic gleam in his eyes.

"It's been a good couple of years, hasn't it?" he said.

"The best decision we ever made was to do this show."

The audience applauded in agreement.

Quinn frowned. "I thought you'd say it was to get married."

"That goes without saying. Who else would have us?"

"That's true. We're hardly the life of the party. We're always in bed by ten..."

Emily had learned long ago to recognize the particularly wicked twinkle in Quinn's eyes just before he said something truly outrageous, and she braced herself.

"And sometimes by nine, if—"

"Quinn!"

"But I will say these days it's no trick at all to get up at four, since we're usually awake, anyway."

Emily glanced toward the edge of the set, where Carrie Lambert stood just out of view of the audience. "We thought you might like to meet the person who's responsible for that," she said, and a hush fell over the studio.

Carrie came across the stage and handed her a small squirmy bundle. Emily fussed for a moment with the elaborate satin and lace christening gown before she held the baby up, shielding her from the brightest of the lights.

And as the camera focused in on her face, Kristen Randolph looked up at her parents and smiled—the very first real smile of her six weeks of life.

Just as if she had been born knowing how to steal a scene, Emily thought. But then, how could their child be any other way?

Let

HARLEQUIN ROMANCE®

take you

BACK TO THE RANCH

**Come to the Bent River Ranch,
near Tulsa, Oklahoma.**

Meet Dusty Dare, owner of one of the most successful cutting-horse ranches in Oklahoma. He's smart, tough, uncompromising—and he's not too happy about hiring a *woman* to run his stables.

Meet Anna Andrews, the woman in question. She's no happier about the situation than Dusty is....

Read DARE TO KISS A COWBOY
by Renee Roszel,
our last Back to the Ranch title. It's a romance that'll make you laugh—and laugh some more!

Available in June wherever Harlequin books are sold.

RANCH13

HARLEQUIN®

Don't miss these Harlequin favorites by some of our most distinguished authors!
And now, you can receive a discount by ordering two or more titles!

HT #25551	THE OTHER WOMAN by Candace Schuler	$2.99	☐
HT #25539	FOOLS RUSH IN by Vicki Lewis Thompson	$2.99	☐
HP #11550	THE GOLDEN GREEK by Sally Wentworth	$2.89	☐
HP #11603	PAST ALL REASON by Kay Thorpe	$2.99	☐
HR #03228	MEANT FOR EACH OTHER by Rebecca Winters	$2.89	☐
HR #03268	THE BAD PENNY by Susan Fox	$2.99	☐
HS #70532	TOUCH THE DAWN by Karen Young	$3.39	☐
HS #70540	FOR THE LOVE OF IVY by Barbara Kaye	$3.39	☐
HI #22177	MINDGAME by Laura Pender	$2.79	☐
HI #22214	TO DIE FOR by M.J. Rodgers	$2.89	☐
HAR #16421	HAPPY NEW YEAR, DARLING by Margaret St. George	$3.29	☐
HAR #16507	THE UNEXPECTED GROOM by Muriel Jensen	$3.50	☐
HH #28774	SPINDRIFT by Miranda Jarrett	$3.99	☐
HH #28782	SWEET SENSATIONS by Julie Tetel	$3.99	☐

Harlequin Promotional Titles

| #83259 | UNTAMED MAVERICK HEARTS | $4.99 | ☐ |

(Short-story collection featuring Heather Graham Pozzessere, Patricia Potter, Joan Johnston)

(limited quantities available on certain titles)

	AMOUNT	$
DEDUCT:	10% DISCOUNT FOR 2+ BOOKS	$
	POSTAGE & HANDLING	$
	($1.00 for one book, 50¢ for each additional)	
	APPLICABLE TAXES*	$ _____
	TOTAL PAYABLE	$ _____
	(check or money order—please do not send cash)	

To order, complete this form and send it, along with a check or money order for the total above, payable to Harlequin Books, to: **In the U.S.:** 3010 Walden Avenue, P.O. Box 9047, Buffalo, NY 14269-9047; **In Canada:** P.O. Box 613, Fort Erie, Ontario, L2A 5X3.

Name: _____

Address: _____ City: _____

State/Prov.: _____ Zip/Postal Code: _____

*New York residents remit applicable sales taxes.
Canadian residents remit applicable GST and provincial taxes.

HBACK-AJ

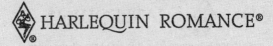 HARLEQUIN ROMANCE®

brings you

Stories that celebrate love, families and children!

Watch for our first Kids & Kisses

**The Baby Battle
by Shannon Waverly
Harlequin Romance #3316**

A deeply emotional Romance centering on the custody battle for a young boy.

Who will be four-year-old Timmy's guardian?

His aunt, Suzanna, who was his mother's sister?

Or his uncle, Logan, a member of the powerful New England family who'd disowned Timmy's father?

Available in June wherever Harlequin books are sold.

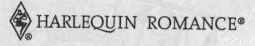
HARLEQUIN ROMANCE®

Question: *What will excite & delight Debbie Macomber's fans?*
Answer: A sequel to her popular 1993 novel,
READY FOR ROMANCE!

Last year you met the two Dryden brothers, Damian and Evan, in
Debbie Macomber's READY FOR ROMANCE. You saw Damian fall in
love with Jessica Kellerman....

Next month watch what happens when Evan discovers that
Mary Jo Summerhill —the love of his life, the woman who'd
rejected him three years before—_isn't_ married, after all!

**Watch for READY FOR MARRIAGE: Harlequin Romance #3307
available in April wherever Harlequin books are sold**

If you missed READY FOR ROMANCE, here's your chance to order:

#03288   READY FOR ROMANCE   Debbie Macomber $2.99 ☐

(limited quantities available)

TOTAL AMOUNT	$	
POSTAGE & HANDLING	$	
($1.00 for one book, 50¢ for each additional)		
APPLICABLE TAXES*	$ _____	
TOTAL PAYABLE	$ _____	
(Send check or money order—please do not send cash)		

To order, complete this form and send it, along with a check or money order for the
total above, payable to Harlequin Books, to: **In the U.S.:** 3010 Walden Avenue,
P.O. Box 9047, Buffalo, NY 14269-9047; **In Canada:** P.O. Box 613, Fort Erie, Ontario,
L2A 5X3.

Name: _____
Address: _____ City: _____
State/Prov.: _____ Zip/Postal Code: _____

*New York residents remit applicable sales taxes.
 Canadian residents remit applicable GST and provincial taxes.

HRRFM

Fifty red-blooded, white-hot, true-blue hunks
from every State in the Union!

Look for MEN MADE IN AMERICA! Written by some of
our most popular authors, these stories feature fifty of
the strongest, sexiest men, each from a different state in
the union!

Two titles available every other month at your favorite
retail outlet.

In May, look for:

LOVE BY PROXY by Diana Palmer (Illinois)
POSSIBLES by Lass Small (Indiana)

In July, look for:

KISS YESTERDAY GOODBYE by Leigh Michaels (Iowa)
A TIME TO KEEP by Curtiss Ann Matlock (Kansas)

You won't be able to resist MEN MADE IN AMERICA!

INDULGE A LITTLE 6947 SWEEPSTAKES
NO PURCHASE NECESSARY

HERE'S HOW THE SWEEPSTAKES WORKS:

The Harlequin Reader Service shipments for January, February and March 1994 will contain, respectively, coupons for entry into three prize drawings: a trip for two to San Francisco, an Alaskan cruise for two and a trip for two to Hawaii. To be eligible for any drawing using an Entry Coupon, simply complete and mail according to directions.

There is no obligation to continue as a Reader Service subscriber to enter and be eligible for any prize drawing. You may also enter any drawing by hand printing your name and address on a 3" x 5" card and the destination of the prize you wish that entry to be considered for (i.e., San Francisco trip, Alaskan cruise or Hawaiian trip). Send your 3" x 5" entries to: Indulge a Little 6947 Sweepstakes, c/o Prize Destination you wish that entry to be considered for, P.O. Box 1315, Buffalo, NY 14269-1315, U.S.A. or Indulge a Little 6947 Sweepstakes, P.O. Box 610, Fort Erie, Ontario L2A 5X3, Canada.

To be eligible for the San Francisco trip, entries must be received by 4/30/94; for the Alaskan cruise, 5/31/94; and the Hawaiian trip, 6/30/94. No responsibility is assumed for lost, late or misdirected mail. Sweepstakes open to residents of the U.S. (except Puerto Rico) and Canada, 18 years of age or older. All applicable laws and regulations apply. Sweepstakes void wherever prohibited.

For a copy of the Official Rules, send a self-addressed, stamped envelope (WA residents need not affix return postage) to: Indulge a Little 6947 Rules, P.O. Box 4631, Blair, NE 68009, U.S.A.

INDR93

INDULGE A LITTLE 6947 SWEEPSTAKES
NO PURCHASE NECESSARY

HERE'S HOW THE SWEEPSTAKES WORKS:

The Harlequin Reader Service shipments for January, February and March 1994 will contain, respectively, coupons for entry into three prize drawings: a trip for two to San Francisco, an Alaskan cruise for two and a trip for two to Hawaii. To be eligible for any drawing using an Entry Coupon, simply complete and mail according to directions.

There is no obligation to continue as a Reader Service subscriber to enter and be eligible for any prize drawing. You may also enter any drawing by hand printing your name and address on a 3" x 5" card and the destination of the prize you wish that entry to be considered for (i.e., San Francisco trip, Alaskan cruise or Hawaiian trip). Send your 3" x 5" entries to: Indulge a Little 6947 Sweepstakes, c/o Prize Destination you wish that entry to be considered for, P.O. Box 1315, Buffalo, NY 14269-1315, U.S.A. or Indulge a Little 6947 Sweepstakes, P.O. Box 610, Fort Erie, Ontario L2A 5X3, Canada.

To be eligible for the San Francisco trip, entries must be received by 4/30/94; for the Alaskan cruise, 5/31/94; and the Hawaiian trip, 6/30/94. No responsibility is assumed for lost, late or misdirected mail. Sweepstakes open to residents of the U.S. (except Puerto Rico) and Canada, 18 years of age or older. All applicable laws and regulations apply. Sweepstakes void wherever prohibited.

For a copy of the Official Rules, send a self-addressed, stamped envelope (WA residents need not affix return postage) to: Indulge a Little 6947 Rules, P.O. Box 4631, Blair, NE 68009, U.S.A.

INDR93

INDULGE A LITTLE
SWEEPSTAKES

OFFICIAL ENTRY COUPON

This entry must be received by: APRIL 30, 1994
This month's winner will be notified by: MAY 15, 1994
Trip must be taken between: JUNE 30, 1994-JUNE 30, 1995

YES, I want to win the San Francisco vacation for two. I understand that the prize includes round-trip airfare, first-class hotel, rental car and pocket money as revealed on the "wallet" scratch-off card.

Name_____

Address _____ Apt. _____

City_____

State/Prov._____ Zip/Postal Code_____

Daytime phone number_____
          (Area Code)

Account #_____

Return entries with invoice in envelope provided. Each book in this shipment has two entry coupons—and the more coupons you enter, the better your chances of winning!
© 1993 HARLEQUIN ENTERPRISES LTD.   MONTH1

INDULGE A LITTLE
SWEEPSTAKES

OFFICIAL ENTRY COUPON

This entry must be received by: APRIL 30, 1994
This month's winner will be notified by: MAY 15, 1994
Trip must be taken between: JUNE 30, 1994-JUNE 30, 1995

YES, I want to win the San Francisco vacation for two. I understand that the prize includes round-trip airfare, first-class hotel, rental car and pocket money as revealed on the "wallet" scratch-off card.

Name_____

Address _____ Apt. _____

City_____

State/Prov._____ Zip/Postal Code_____

Daytime phone number_____
          (Area Code)

Account #_____

Return entries with invoice in envelope provided. Each book in this shipment has two entry coupons—and the more coupons you enter, the better your chances of winning!
© 1993 HARLEQUIN ENTERPRISES LTD.   MONTH1